GW00480657

WH

FURS:

MY LIFE AS A BON VIVANT, GAMBLER & LOVE RAT

BY

JESUS H. CHRIST

EDITED AND INTRODUCED BY

STEWART HOME

ATTACK! is an imprint of Creation books

First published in 2000 by ATTACK! Books
www.creationbooks.com
Copyright: Jesus H. Christ 2000 AD
Design by Rom
Original artwork by Paul McAffery
Printed and bound in Great Britain by
Woolnough Bookbinding Ltd
Irthlingborough, Northants

Jesus H. Christ either lives in heaven with his dad. Or he doesn't.

Stewart Home has written loads of books. He is the world's top modern artist and a totally unreconstructed punk rock musician.

Will Self once described Stewart as an "nasty" little skinhead".

Stewart wishes to make known that this is bollocks and that Mr. Self is a "twat".

"If one defines "little" as "lacking physical stature relative to the gender-specific national average" then I'm not "little" at all, you gawky, Oxbridge junkie wanker!" snarls Stewart.

Stewart either lives in east London with a runaway teenage creack ho whom he pimps. Or he doesn't.

WHIPS & FURS:
MY LIFE AS A BON VIVANT, GAMBLER & LOVE RAT

BY JESUS H. CHRIST
edited and introduced by Stewart Home

INTRODUCTION

I dunno, maybe it was the many months I'd spent seeking mystic inspiration from the bottom of bottles of finest Springbank single malt whisky; or perhaps it was Kelly who lived next door (with, I might add, a menagerie of pet ferrets), who kept offering to jerk me off. Each time I accepted the offer of a sultry hand job, Kelly would run away after half completing the sexual favour, causing me to fall flat on my face when I jumped up and tried to give chase. I'm useless at running with my trousers around my ankles. Regardless, I knew the repeated concussions I'd suffered had aided my quest for the truth about the historical Jesus. Thus it was that I came round one night convinced that Jesus had written an autobiography which I'd find on the Internet.

> After getting up gingerly and washing blood from my hands, I called down a search engine on my Mac. Since I knew intuitively that any genuine information about Jesus was bound to be disguised to prevent its suppression by self-interested parties (Ling masters, Protestant iconoclasts, short order pastry cooks etc.), I decided to look for something that appeared to be about the Victorian speculator Cecil Rhodes. It didn't take me long to come up with the goods I required. Thanks to my sophisticated knowledge of codes and word substitutions (which had been much improved through amnesia), the quest for the historical Jesus was over. Indeed, Christ stood revealed as a very human figure (which might come as a bit of a shock to

docetists but offers real support for the opposed heresy of Arianism). It goes without saying that Jesus should be judged by the standards of his own time, but I would like to emphasise that rape is not something to be taken lightly. You wouldn't like it if you or your friends were subjected to a sexual assault. The fantasies that follow are clearly pathological, as well as pathetic. Fortunately, they've become less acceptable today than they were twenty-five or thirty years ago. Likewise, while their ontological status is dubious, this does not necessarily decrease the offense aroused by representations of this type (particularly in Protestant cultures with their long traditions of iconoclasm).

What follows is not only extremely distasteful, I would also question the authenticity of the sexual element within this sick narrative. Among other things, it is well known that camels have one of the highest pain thresholds of all mammals. In Whips & Furs: My life as a bon-vivant, gambler & love rat by Jesus H. Christ, the identical descriptions of a woman and a camel being flagellated indicate either a lack of knowledge on the part of the author (making it unlikely he has ever engaged in sexual relations with a camel), or else an interest in the deconstruction of Orientalised pornographic fantasies (making it unnecessary for the author to have a first-hand knowledge of camel sex). Either way, the believability of the sexual passages must be called into question. I rather suspect that these incidents have been interpolated by a writer other than Jesus H. Christ. The reader will have to make up their own mind about this. However, it should not pass unremarked that these sex scenes bear an astonishing similarity to what has been reprinted and marketed over recent years as "Victorian erotica". That said, the fact that there is nothing classic about this misogynist crap does not invalidate the main thrust of Jesus H. Christ's narrative. Regardless of whether what follows has any historical validity whatsoever, if the sex scenes are ignored it is undoubtedly a rollicking good read. It is also more credible than The Bible, which is blatantly contradictory and was standardised years after the event by a bunch of bureaucrats known as the Council of Nicaea. The Bible also includes a great deal more rape, murder and general unpleasantness than the present tome (no wonder it is an international bestseller). By way of conclusion, please send me your love offerings (c/o Attack Books) in the form of cheques made payable to CASH. Linguistics is the science that puts hairs on your chest. Mine is a double. Cheers.

Stewart Home, London January 2000.

CHAPTER ONE

My name is Jesus H. Christ. I am brother-in-law and secretary to Judas Iscariot, the famous camel trader. Many years ago, when Judas Iscariot was a short change artist in Damascus, I had the (qualified) good fortune to marry his sister. Much later, when the Iscariot estate and farm near Nazareth developed by degrees into the biggest camel dealership in the Roman Empire, my brother-in-law offered me the not unremunerative post of secretary, in which capacity I have ever since been his constant and attached companion.

He is not a man whom any common sharper can take in, is Judas Iscariot. Middle height, square build, firm mouth, keen eyes - the very picture of a smart and successful business genius. I have only known one rogue impose upon Judas, and that one knave, as the Commissary of Police at Samaria remarked, would doubtless have imposed upon a syndicate of Satan, Lucifer and Mephistopheles.

We had run across to the Mediterranean for a few weeks in the season. Our object being strictly rest and recreation from the arduous duties of camel trading, we did not think it necessary to take our wives out with us. Indeed, Lady Iscariot is absolutely wedded to the joys of Bethlehem, and does not appreciate the rural delights of the Mediterranean littoral. But Judas and I, though immersed in affairs when at home, both thoroughly enjoy the complete change from the city to the charming vegetation and pellucid air on the terrace at Palermo. We are so fond of scenery. That delicious view over the rocks of Palermo, with some nice mountains in the rear, and the blue sea in front, not to mention the imposing slave market in the foreground, appeals to me as one of the most beautiful prospects in the Roman Empire and freshens him, after the turmoil of Bethlehem, to win a few hundreds at dice in the course of an afternoon, among the palms and cactuses and pure breezes of Palermo. The place, say I, for a jaded intellect! However, we never on any account actually stop on the island itself. Judas thinks Palermo is not a sound address for a trader's letters. He prefers a comfortable inn near the harbour at Naples, where he recovers health and renovates his nervous system by taking daily excursions along the coast.

This particular season we were snugly ensconced at the Romulus Inn. We had capital quarters on the first floor - salon, study, and bedrooms - and found on the spot a most agreeable cosmopolitan society. All Naples, just then, was ringing with talk about a curious impostor, known to his followers as the Great Druid Seer, and supposed to be gifted with second sight, as well as with endless other supernatural powers. Now, it is a peculiarity of my able brother-in-law's that, when he meets with a quack, he burns to expose him, he is so keen a man of business himself that it gives him, so to speak, a disinterested pleasure to unmask and detect imposture in others. Many ladies at the inn, some of whom had met and conversed with the Druid Seer, were constantly telling us strange stories of his doings - he had disclosed to one the present whereabouts of a runaway husband, he had pointed out to another the numbers that would win at dice next evening, he had shown a third the image on a screen of the man she had for years adored without his knowledge. Of course, Judas didn't believe a word of it, but his curiosity was roused, he wished to see and judge for himself of the wonderful thought-reader.

'What would be his terms, do you think, for a private seance,' he asked of Madame Picardet, the lady to whom the Seer had successfully predicted the winning numbers.

'He does not work for money,' Madame Picardet answered, 'but for the good of humanity. I'm sure he would gladly come and exhibit for nothing his miraculous faculties.'

'Nonsense!' Judas answered. 'The man must live. I'd pay him five minas, though, to see him alone. What inn is he stopping at?'

'The Drunken Frog, I think,' the lady answered. 'Oh no,

I remember now, the Boar's Head.'

Judas turned to me quietly. 'Look here, Jesus,' he whispered. 'Go round to this fellow's place immediately after dinner, and offer him five minas to give a private seance at once in my rooms without mentioning who I am to him, keep the name quite quiet. Bring him back with you, too, and come straight upstairs with him, so that there may be no collusion. We'll see just how much the fellow can tell us.'

I went, as directed. I found the Seer a very remarkable and interesting person. He stood about Judas's own height, but was slimmer and straighter, with an aquiline nose, strangely piercing eyes, very large, black pupils, and a finely-chiselled, close-shaven face like the bust of Antinous in our sitting room back home. What gave him his most characteristic touch, however, was his odd head of hair, curly and wavy like Ham's, standing out in a halo round his high white forehead and his delicate profile. I could see at a glance why he succeeded so well in impressing women: he had the look of a poet, a singer, a prophet.

'I have come round,' I said, 'to ask whether you will consent to give a seance at once in a friend's rooms, and my principal wishes me to add that he is prepared to pay five minas as the price of the entertainment.'

Laird Archibald McArchibald, that was what he called himself, bowed to me with impressive Scottish politeness. His rosy blushed cheeks were wrinkled with a smile of gentle contempt as he answered, gravely: 'I do not sell my gifts, I bestow them freely. If your friend - your anonymous friend - desires to behold the cosmic wonders that are wrought through my hands, I am glad to show them to him. Fortunately, as often happens when it is necessary to convince and confound a sceptic (for that our friend is a sceptic I feel instinctively), I chance to have no engagements at all this evening.' He ran his hand through his fine, long hair, reflectively. 'Yes, I go,' he continued, as if addressing some unknown presence that hovered about the ceiling, 'I go, come with me!' Then he put on his broad sword, with its crimson ribbon showing it was used principally for Highland dancing, wrapped a plaid cloak round his shoulders, and strode forth by my side towards a meeting with my brother-in-law Judas Iscariot.

He talked little by the way, and that little in curt sentences. He seemed buried in deep thought, indeed, when we reached the door and I turned in, he walked a step or two further on, as if not noticing to what place I had brought him. Then he drew himself up short, and gazed around him for a moment.

' Ha, the Hebrews,' he said - and I may mention in passing that his Latin, in spite of a slight northern accent, was idiomatic and excellent. 'It is here, then, it is here!' He was addressing once more the unseen presence.

I smiled to think that these childish devices were intended to deceive Judas Iscariot. Not quite the sort of man (as the people of Bethlehem know) to be taken in by hocus-pocus. And all this, I saw, was the cheapest and most commonplace conjurer's patter.

We went upstairs to our rooms. Judas had gathered together a few friends to watch the performance. The Seer entered, wrapped in thought. He was dressed in white robes, but a red sash round his waist gave a touch of picturesqueness and a dash of colour. He paused for a moment in the middle of the salon without letting his eyes rest on anybody or anything. Then he walked straight up to Judas and held out his dark hand.

'Good evening,' he said. 'You are the host. My soul's sight tells me so.'

'Good shot,' Judas answered. 'These fellows have to be quick-witted, you know, Mrs. MacKenzie, or they'd never get on at it.'

The Seer gazed about him, and smiled blankly at a person or two whose faces he seemed to recognise from a previous existence. Then Judas began to ask him a few simple questions, not about himself, but about me, just to test him. He answered most of them with surprising correctness. 'His name? His name begins with an J, I think. You call him Jesus' He paused long between each clause, as if the facts were revealed to him slowly. 'Jesus - Christ - The Son of King David. No, not King David! Jesus H. Christ. There seems to be some connection in somebody's mind now present between Christ and King David. I am not an Essene. I do not know what it means. But they are somehow the same name, Jesus and King David.'

He gazed around apparently for confirmation. A lady came to his rescue. 'All the generations from Abraham to David are fourteen generations, and from David until the carrying away into Babylon are fourteen generations, and from the carrying away into Babylon unto Christ are fourteen generations,' she murmured, gently, 'and I was wondering, as you spoke, whether Mr. Christ here might possibly be descended from David and ultimately Abraham.'

'He is,' the Seer replied, instantly, with a flash of those blue eyes. And I thought this curious: for though my father always maintained the reality of the relationship, there was one link wanting to complete the pedigree. He could not be sure that Matthan was the father of Jacob, the Red Sea shaman who after eating psychedelic mushrooms saw a ladder and reached heaven by climbing up his own hallucination.

'Where was he born?' Judas interrupted.

The Seer clapped his two hands to his forehead and held it between them, as if to prevent it from bursting. 'Palestine,' he said, slowly, as the facts narrowed down, so to speak. 'Judaea, Bethlehem, in the stables of an inn, he was born in a manger.'

'By Moses, he's correct,' Judas muttered. 'He seems really to do it. Still, he may have found Jez out. He may have asked him on the way over here.'

'I never gave a hint,' I answered, 'till he reached the door, he didn't even know to what inn I was piloting him.'

The Seer stroked his chin softly. His eye appeared to me to have a furtive gleam in it. 'Would you like me to tell you the value of several pieces of silver enclosed in an envelope?' he asked, casually.

'Go out of the room,' Judas said, 'while I pass it round the company.'

Laird McArchibald disappeared. Judas passed the silver, just one coin, round cautiously, holding it all the time in his own hand, but letting his guests see the single coin. Then he placed it in an envelope and gummed it down firmly.

The Seer returned. His keen eyes swept the company with a comprehensive glance. He shook his shaggy mane. Then he took the envelope in his hands and gazed at it fixedly. 'Nero's Head' he answered, in a slow tone. 'A Roman coin for fifty minas - exchanged at the slave market for gold won yesterday at Palermo.'

'I see how he did that,' Judas said, triumphantly. 'He must have changed it there himself, and then I changed it back again. In point of fact, I remember seeing a fellow with long hair loafing about. Still, it's capital conjuring.'

'He can see through matter,' one of the ladies interposed. It was Madame Picardet. 'He can see through a box.' She drew a little gold vinaigrette, such as our grandmothers used, from her dress-pocket. 'What is in this?' she inquired, holding it up to him.

Laird McArchibald gazed through it. 'Three gold coins,' he replied, knitting his brows with the effort of seeing into the box:.

She opened the box and passed it round. Judas smiled a quiet smile.

'Confederacy!' he muttered, half to himself. 'Confederacy!'

The Seer turned to him with a sullen air. 'You want a better sign?' he said, in a very impressive voice. 'A sign that will convince you! Very well. You have a letter in your left waistcoat pocket, a crumpled-up letter. Do you wish me to read it out? I will, if you desire it.'

It may seem to those who know Judas incredible, but, I am bound to admit, my brother-in-law coloured. What that letter contained, I cannot say, he only answered, very testily and evasively, 'No, thank you, I won't trouble you. The exhibition you have already given us of your skill in this kind more than amply suffices.' And his fingers strayed nervously to his waistcoat pocket, as if he was half afraid, even then Laird McArchibald would read it.

I fancied, too, he glanced somewhat anxiously towards Madame Picardet.

The Seer bowed courteously. 'Your will Jimmy boy, is law,' he said. 'I make it a principle, though I can see through all things, invariably to respect secrecy and sanctities. If it were not so, I might dissolve society. For which of us is there who could bear the whole truth being told about him?' He gazed around the room. An unpleasant thrill supervened. Most of us felt this uncanny Celtic Druid knew really too much. And some of us were engaged in trading swindles.

'For example,' the Seer continued, blandly, 'I happened a few weeks ago to travel down here from Florence by mule train with a very intelligent man, a Roman official and part time trader. He had in his bag some documents, some confidential documents:' he glanced at Judas. 'You know the kind of thing, my dear. Reports from experts, from vetinary surgeons. You may have seen some such, marked, STRICTLY PRIVATE.'

'They form an element in camel trading,' Judas admitted, coldly.

' Precisely,' the Seer murmured, his accent for a moment less Scottish than before. 'And, as they were marked strictly private, I respect, of course, the seal of confidence. That's all I wish to say. I hold it a duty, being entrusted with such powers, not to use them in a manner which may annoy or incommode my fellow creatures.'

'Your feeling does you honour,' Judas answered, with some acerbity. Then he whispered in my ear: 'Confounded clever scoundrel, Jez, rather wish we hadn't brought him here.'

Laird McArchibald seemed intuitively to divine this wish, for he interposed, in a lighter and gayer tone: 'I will now show you a different and more interesting embodiment of occult power, for which we shall need a somewhat subdued arrangement of surrounding lights. Would you mind, Jimmy boy - for I have purposely abstained from reading your name on the brain of anyone present - would you mind my turning down this lamp just a little? So! That will do. Now, this one, and this one. Exactly! That's right.' He poured a few grains of powder out of a packet into a saucer. 'Next, a light, if you please. Thank you!' It burnt with a strange green light. He drew from his pocket a card, and produced some ink. 'Have you a quill?' he asked.

I instantly brought one. He handed it to Judas. 'Oblige me,' he said, 'by writing your name there.' And he indicated a place in the centre of the card, which had an embossed edge, with a small middle square of a different colour.

Judas has a natural disinclination to signing his name without knowing why. What do you want with it?' he asked. (A camel trader's signature has so many uses.)

'I want you to put the card in an envelope,' the Seer replied, 'and then to burn it. After that, I shall show you your own name written in letters of blood on my arm, in your own handwriting.'

Judas took the quill. If the signature was to be burned as soon as written, he didn't mind giving it. He wrote his name in his usual firm, clear style, the writing of a man who knows his worth and is not afraid of signing away the deeds for a banana plantation.

'Look at it long,' the Seer said, from the other side of the room. He had not watched him write it.

Judas stared at it fixedly. The Seer was really beginning to produce an impression.

'Now, put it in that envelope,' the Seer exclaimed.

Judas, like a lamb, placed it as directed.

The Seer strode forward. 'Give me the envelope,' he said. He took it in his hand, walked over towards the fire-place, and solemnly burnt it. 'See, it crumbles into ashes,' he cried. Then he came back to the middle of the room, close to the green light, rolled up his sleeve, and held his arm before Judas. There, in blood-red letters, my brother-in-law read the name, 'Judas Iscariot,' in his own handwriting!

'I see how that's done,' Judas murmured, drawing back. 'It's a clever delusion, but still, I see through it. It's like that ghost-book. Your ink was deep green, your light was green, you made me look at it long, and then I saw the same thing written on the skin of your arm in complementary colours.'

'You think so?' the Seer replied, with a curious curl of the lip.

'I'm sure of it,' Judas answered.

Quick as lightning, the Seer again rolled up his sleeve. 'That's your name,' he cried, in a very clear voice, 'but not your whole name. What do you say, then, to my right? Is this one also a complementary colour?' He held his other arm out. There, in sea-green letters, I read the name, 'Judas Eliphaz Iscariot.' It is my brother-in-law's full designation, but he has dropped the Eliphaz for many years past, and, to say the truth, doesn't like it. He is a little bit ashamed of his mother's family.

Judas glanced at it hurriedly. 'Quite right,' he said, 'quite right!' But his voice was hollow. I could guess he didn't care to continue the seance. He could see through the man, of course, but it was clear the fellow knew too much about us to be entirely pleasant.

'Turn up the lights,' I said, and a servant turned them. 'Shall I say wine and benediction?' I whispered to Iscariot.

'By all means,' he answered. 'Anything to keep this fellow from further impertinences! And, I say, don't you think you'd better suggest at the same time that the men should smoke? Even these ladies are not above inhaling the smoke from banana skins, some of them.'

There was a sigh of relief. The lights burned brightly. The Seer for the moment retired from business, so to speak. He accepted a drink with a very good grace, sipped his wine in a corner, and chatted to the lady who had suggested King David with marked politeness. He was a polished knave.

Next morning, in the hall of the inn, I saw Madame Picardet again, in a neat travelling robe, evidently bound for a ship.

'What, off, Madame Picardet?' I cried.

She smiled, and held out her prettily-gloved hand. 'Yes, I'm off,' she answered, archly. 'Florence, or Turin, or somewhere. I've drained Naples dry, like a sucked orange. Got all the fun I can out of it. Now I'm away again to my beloved Northern Italy.'

But it struck me as odd that, if the North was her game, she was boarding a ship that was heading South. However, a man of the world accepts what a lady tells him, no matter how improbable, and I confess, for ten days or so, I thought no more about her, or the Seer either.

At the end of that time, our fortnight pass-book came in from my money lender in Bethlehem. It is part of my duty, as the camel trader's secretary, to make up this book once a fortnight, and to compare the cancelled credit notes with Judas's counterfoils. On this particular occasion, I happened to observe what I can only describe as a very grave discrepancy. In fact, a discrepancy of 5,000 minas. On the wrong side, too. Judas was debited with 5,000 minas more than the total amount that was shown on the counterfoils.

I examined the book with care. The source of the error was obvious. It lay in a cheque to Self or Bearer, for 5,000 minas, signed by Judas, and evidently paid across the counter in Bethlehem, as it bore on its face no stamp or indication of any other office.

I called in my brother-in-law from the salon to the study. 'Look here, Judas,' I said, 'there's a credit note in the book which you haven't entered.' And I handed it to him without comment, for I thought it might have been drawn to settle some little loss on the turf or at cards, or to make up some other affair he didn't desire to mention to me. These things will happen.

He looked at it and stared hard. Then he pursed up his mouth and gave a long low 'Whew!' At last he turned it over and remarked, 'I say, Jez, my boy, we've just been done jolly well brown, haven't we?'

I glanced at the cheque. 'How do you mean?' I inquired.

'Why, the Seer,' he replied, still staring at it ruefully. 'I don't mind the five thousand, but to think the fellow should have gammoned the pair of us like that. Ignominious, I call it!'

'How do you know it's the Seer?' I asked.

'Look at the green ink,' he answered. 'Besides, I recollect the very shape of the last flourish. I flourished a bit like that in the excitement of the moment, which I don't always do with my regular signature.'

'He's done us,' I answered, recognising it. 'But how the hell did he manage to transfer it to the credit note? This looks like your own handwriting, Judas, not a clever forgery.'

'It is,' he said. 'I admit it, I can't deny it. Only fancy his bamboozling me when I was most on my guard! I wasn't to be taken in by any of his silly occult tricks and catch-words, but it never occurred to me he was going to victimise me financially in this way. I expected attempts at a loan or an extortion, but to collar my signature to a blank credit note, atrocious!'

'How did he manage it?' I asked.

'I haven't the faintest conception. I only know those are the words I wrote. I could swear to them anywhere.'

'Then you can't protest the credit note?'

'Unfortunately, no, it's my own true signature.'

We went that afternoon without delay to see the Chief Commissary of Police at his office. He was a gentlemanly Gaul much less formal and red-tapey than usual, and he spoke excellent Latin, with a Breton accent, having acted, in fact, as a detective amongst the Celts for about ten years in his early manhood.

'I guess,' he said slowly, after hearing our story, 'you've been victimised right here by Arugath ha-Bosem, gentlemen.'

'Who is Arugath ha-Bosem ? ' Judas asked.

'That's just what I want to know,' the Commissary answered, in his curious Breton-French-Latin. 'He is an Arugath, because he deceives everyone who crosses his path, he is called

Arugath ha-Bosem, because he teaches his victims the difference between appearance and reality. He can mould his face like clay in the hands of a potter. Real name, unknown. Nationality, equally Hebrew and Arabic. Address, usually Philistia. Profession, former maker of wax figures to the Epicureans for use in bizarre sexual practices. Age, what he chooses. Employs his knowledge to mould his own nose and cheeks, with wax additions to the character he decides to impersonate. Aquiline, this time, you say! Anything like these drawings?'

He rummaged in his desk and handed us two.

'Not in the least,' Judas answered, 'except perhaps, as to the neck, everything here is quite unlike him.'

'Then that's Arugath!' the Commissary answered with decision, rubbing his hands in glee. 'Look here,' and he took out a quill and rapidly sketched the outline of one of the two faces, that of a bland looking young man, with no expression worth mentioning. 'There's Arugath in his simple disguise. Very good. Now watch me. Figure to yourself that he adds here a tiny patch of wax to his nose - an aquiline bridge - just so, well, you have him right there, and the chin, ah, one touch: now, for hair, a wig: for complexion, nothing easier: that's the profile of your rascal, isn't it?'

'Exactly,' we both murmured. By two curves of the quill, and a shock of false hair, the face was transmuted.

'He had very large eyes, with very big pupils, though,' I objected, looking close 'and the man in the picture here has them small and boiled-fishy.'

'That's so,' the Commissary answered. 'A drop of belladonna expands and produce the Seer. Five grains of opium contracts and give a dead-alive, stupidly-innocent appearance. Well, you leave this affair to me, gentlemen. I'll see the fun out. I don't say I'll catch him for you, nobody ever yet has caught Arugath ha-Bosem, but I'll explain how he did the trick, and that ought to be consolation enough to a man of your means for a trifle of five thousand!'

'You are not the conventional Roman office-holder,' I

ventured to interpose.

'You bet!' the Commissary replied, and drew himself up like a captain of several legions. 'Sirs,' he continued, in Latin, with the utmost dignity, 'I shall devote the resources of this office to tracing out the crime, and, if possible, to effectuating the arrest of the culpable.'

We telegraphed to Bethlehem, of course, and we wrote to the money lender, with a full description of the suspected person. But I need hardly add that nothing came of it.

Three days later, the Commissary called at our inn. Well, gentlemen,' he said, ' I am glad to say I have discovered everything!'

'What? Arrested the Seer?' Judas cried.

The Commissary drew back, almost horrified at the suggestion.

'Arrested Arugath ha-Bosem?' he exclaimed. 'Fuck me, we are only human! Arrested him? No, not quite. But tracked out how he did it. That is already much. To unravel Arugath ha-Bosem, gentlemen!'

'Well, what do you make of it?' Judas asked, crestfallen.

The Commissary sat down and gloated over his discovery. It was clear a well-planned crime amused him vastly. 'In the first place, mister,' he said, 'disabuse your mind of the idea that when Christ your secretary went out to fetch Laird McArchibald that night, Laird McArchibald didn't know to whose rooms he was going. Quite otherwise, in point of fact. I do not doubt myself that Laird McArchibald, or Arugath ha-Bosem (call him which you like), came to Naples this winter for no other purpose than just to rob you.'

'But I sent for him,' my brother-in-law interposed.

'Yes, he meant you to send for him. He forced a card, so to speak. If he couldn't do that, I guess he would be a pretty poor conjurer. He had a lady of his own - his wife, let us say, or his sister - stopping here at this inn, a certain Madame Picardet. Through her, he induced several ladies of your circle to attend his seances. She and they spoke to you about him, and aroused your curiosity. You may bet your last shekel that when he came to this room, he came ready primed and prepared with endless facts about both of you.'

'What fools we have been, Jez,' my brother-in-law exclaimed.' I see it all now. That designing woman sent round before dinner to say I wanted to meet him, and by the time you got there, he was ready for bamboozling me.'

'That's so,' the Commissary answered. 'He had your name ready painted on both his arms, and he had made other preparations of still greater importance.'

'You mean the credit note. Well, how did he get it?'

The Commissary opened the door. 'Come in,' he said. And a young man entered whom we recognised at once as the chief clerk of the money lender we dealt with in Naples.

'State what you know of this credit note,' the Commissary said, showing it to him, for we had handed it over to the police as a piece of evidence.

'About four weeks since...' the clerk began.

'Say ten days before your seance,' the Commissary interposed.

'A gentleman with very long hair and an aquiline nose, dark, strange, and handsome, called in at my department and asked if I could tell him the name of Judas Iscariot's Bethlehem money lender. He said he had a sum to pay in to your credit, and asked if we would forward it for him. I told him it was irregular for us to receive the money, as you had no account with us, but that your Bethlehem money lender was called Rothenberg...'

'Quite right,' Judas murmured.

'Two days later a lady, Madame Picardet, who was a customer of ours, brought in a good cheque for three hundred minas, signed by a first-rate name, and asked us to pay it in on her behalf to Rothenberg, and to open a Bethlehem account with them for her. We did so, and received in reply several blank credit notes.'

'From amongst which this credit note was taken, as I learnt from the number, by messenger from Bethlehem,' the

Commissary put in. 'Also, that on the same day on which your cheque was cashed, Madame Picardet, in Bethlehem withdrew her balance.'

'But how did the fellow get me to sign the cheque?' Judas cried. 'How did he manage the card trick?'

The Commissary produced a similar card from his pocket. 'Was that the sort of thing?' he asked.

'Precisely! A facsimile.'

'I thought so. Well, our Arugath, I find, bought a packet of such cards, intended for admission to a religious function, at a market stall. He cut out the centre, and, see here...' The Commissary turned it over, and showed a piece of paper pasted neatly over the back, this he tore off, and there, concealed behind it, lay a folded credit note, with only the place where the signature should be written showing through on the face which the Seer had presented to us. 'I call that a neat trick,' the Commissary remarked, with professional enjoyment of a really good deception.

'But he burnt the envelope before my eyes,' Judas exclaimed.

'Pooh!' the Commissary answered. 'What would he be worth as a conjurer anyway, if he couldn't substitute one envelope for another between the table and the fireplace without your noticing it? And Arugath ha-Bosem, you must remember, is a prince among conjurers.'

Well, it's a comfort to know we've identified our man, and the woman who was with him,' Judas said, with a slight sigh of relief. 'The next thing will be, of course, you'll follow them up on these clues in Bethlehem and arrest them?'

The Commissary shrugged his shoulders. 'Arrest them!' he exclaimed, much amused. 'Ah, mister, but you are sanguine! No officer of justice has ever succeeded in arresting le Arugath Caoutchouc, as they call him in Gaul. He is as slippery as an eel, that man. He wriggles through our fingers. Suppose even we caught him, what could we prove? I ask you. Nobody who has seen him once can ever swear to him again in his next impersonation. He is 'impossible,' this good Arugath. On the day when I arrest him, I assure you, mister, I shall consider myself the smartest police-officer in the Roman Empire.'

'Well, I shall catch him yet,' Judas answered, and relapsed into silence.

CHAPTER TWO

While we were in Naples, Judas was presented with a Grecian maid by a rich Roman citizen who wanted some advice about buying camels. Judas has a mortal fear of catching the clap, and although he was assured that the love slave gifted to him was a certified virgin, he ordered me to get a doctor to examine her. I'd taken rather a fancy to this particular piece of maiden tribute, so I hired an old whore and got a physician to examine the middle-aged harlot and then brought the doctor before my employer to present his report.

'She's disease ridden.' the physician told Judas, 'I wouldn't touch her with your dick.'

Judas was disgusted and told me to do whatever I pleased with the Grecian slave, and I'm pleased to say, I found her a pure maid, her virginity I sacrificed on the feast of our Holy Prophet Moses. To cull her sweet flower, I was obliged to infuse an opiate in her wine. Again and again, I offered thanks to the honest Roman citizen for this gift - her beauties were indeed luxurious, in her soft embraces I found a sure solace from the anxieties of my station, how strange it was that slaves, whose destinies depended on my master's will, rarely gave the fervent return to my pleasure so absolutely necessary to full voluptuous enjoyment. It is true nature will always exert its power over the softer sex, and they frequently give way to its excitement, but the pleasure they experience is merely animal. Thus it was with Mary (I decided to name the Grecian slave girl after my wife): even in the height of our ecstasies, a cloud seemed to hang on her beauteous countenance, clearly indicating that it is nature, not love, that created her transport.

This knowledge considerably diminished the enjoyment her beauties afforded me, yet still she became extremely necessary to my pleasures. Although the novelty of her charms wore thin, the certainty of having cropped her virgin rose created a lasting interest in my breast, which the dissolving lustre and modest, bashful expression of her eyes daily increased - indeed her charms frequently enticed me from the arms of another beauty, who up to that time I had been enjoying throughout my sojourn in Naples without the least abatement of my ardour - on the contrary, my appetite seemed to increase by what I fed upon. It is true when I thought of the pensive charms of Mary I devoted a few hours to her arms, but she only acted like the whetstone to a knife and sent me back to the embraces of my Roman whore with redoubled vigour and zest.

CHAPTER THREE

'Let us take a trip to Jordan,' said Lady Iscariot. And anyone who knows Martha will not be surprised to learn that we did take a trip to Jordan accordingly. Nobody can drive Judas except his wife. And nobody at all can drive Martha.

There were difficulties at the outset, because we had not ordered rooms at the inn beforehand, and it was well on in the season, but they were overcome at last by the usual application of a golden key, and we found ourselves in due time pleasantly quartered in Amman, at that most comfortable of Palestinian hostelries, The Oriental.

We were a square party of four. Judas and Martha, myself and Mary. We had nice big rooms, on the first floor overlooking a lake, and as none of us was possessed with the faintest symptom of that incipient mania which shows itself in the form of an insane desire to trek needlessly across the desert, I will venture to assert we all enjoyed ourselves. We spent most of our time sensibly in lounging about the lake on jolly little sailing ships, and when we did a trek in the desert, it was on camels where these beasts undertook all the muscular work for us.

As usual, at the inn, a great many miscellaneous people showed a burning desire to be specially nice to us. If you wish to see how friendly and charming humanity is, just try being a well-known camel trader for a week, and you'll learn a thing or two. Wherever Judas goes, he is surrounded by charming and disinterested people, all eager to make his distinguished acquaintance, and all familiar with several excellent trading opportunities or several deserving objects of charity. It is my business in life, as his brother-in-law and secretary, to decline with thanks the excellent offers of trade, and to throw judicious cold water on the objects of charity. Even I myself, as the great man's almoner, am very much sought after. People casually allude before me to artless stories of 'poor rabbis in Ramah, you know, Mr. Christ,' or widows in Gophna, penniless Kabalists with the key to Hekhaloth in their desks, and young Golem masters who need but the breath of a patron to open to them the doors of an admiring rabbinical authority. I smile and look wise while I administer cold water in minute doses, but I never report one of these cases to Judas, except in the rare or almost unheard-of event where I think there is really something in them.

Ever since our little adventure with the Druid Seer at Naples, Judas, who is constitutionally cautious, had been even more careful than usual about possible sharpers. And, as chance would have it, there sat just opposite us at the table d'hote at The Oriental - 'tis a fad of Martha's to dine at table d'hote, she says she can't bear to be boxed up all day in private rooms with 'too much family' - a sinister-looking man with fair hair and blue eyes, conspicuous by his bushy, overhanging eyebrows. My attention was first called to the eyebrows in question by a nice little rabbi who sat at our side, and who observed that they were made up of certain large and bristly hairs, which (he told us) had been traced by John The Baptist to our monkey ancestors. Very pleasant little fellow, this fresh-faced young rabbi, on his honeymoon tour with a nice wee wife, a bonnie Syrian lassie with a charming accent.

I looked at the eyebrows close. Then a sudden thought struck me. 'Do you believe they're his own?' I asked of the rabbi, 'or are they only stuck on, a make-up disguise? They really almost look like it.'

You don't suppose?' Judas began, and checked himself suddenly.

'Yes, I do,' I answered, 'the Seer!' Then I recollected my blunder, and looked down sheepishly. For, to say the truth, Iscariot had straightly enjoined on me long before to say nothing of our painful little episode at Naples to Martha, he was afraid if she once heard of it, he would hear of it for ever after.

'What Seer?' the little rabbi inquired, with theological curiosity.

I noticed the man with the overhanging eyebrows give a queer sort of start. Judas's glance was fixed upon me. I hardly knew what to answer.

'Oh, a man who was at Naples with us last year,' I stammered out, trying hard to look unconcerned. 'A fellow they talked about, that's all.' And I turned the subject.

But the rabbi, like a donkey, wouldn't let me turn it.

'Had he eyebrows like that?' he inquired, in an undertone.

I was really angry. If this was Arugath ha-Bosem, the rabbi was obviously giving him the cue, and making it much more difficult for us to catch him, now we might possibly have lighted on the chance of doing so.

'No, he hadn't,' I answered, testily, 'it was a passing expression. But this is not the man. I was mistaken, no doubt.' And I nudged him gently.

The little rabbi was too innocent for anything. 'Oh, I see,' he replied, nodding hard and looking wise. Then he turned to his wife, and made an obvious face, which the man with the eyebrows couldn't fail to notice.

Fortunately, a political discussion going on a few places further down the table spread up to us and diverted attention for a moment. The magical name of Julius Caesar saved us. Judas flared up. I was truly pleased, for I could see Martha was boiling over with curiosity by this time.

After dinner, in the dice-room, however, the man with the big eyebrows sidled up and began to talk to me. If he was Arugath ha-Bosem, it was evident he bore us no grudge at all for the five thousand minas he had done us out of. On the contrary, he seemed quite prepared to do us out of five thousand more when opportunity offered, for he introduced himself at once as Dr. Hector MacPherson, the exclusive grantee of extensive concessions from the Celtic Tribal Elders on the Upper Donside. He dived into conversation with me at once as to the splendid mineral resources of his Scottish estate - the silver, the platinum, the actual rubies, the possible diamonds. I listened and smiled, I knew what was coming. All he needed to develop this magnificent concession was a little more capital. It was sad to see thousands of minas' worth of platinum and cart-loads of rubies just crumbling in the soil or carried away by the river, for want of a few hundred to work them with properly. If he knew of anybody, now, with money to invest, he could recommend him - nay, offer him - a unique opportunity of earning, say, forty per cent on his capital, on unimpeachable security.

'I wouldn't do it for every man,' Dr. Hector MacPherson remarked, drawing himself up, 'but if I took a fancy to a fellow who had command of ready cash, I might choose to put him in the way of feathering his nest with unexampled rapidity.'

'Exceedingly disinterested of you,' I answered, dryly, fixing my eyes on his eyebrows.

The little rabbi, meanwhile, was playing dice with Judas. His glance followed mine as it rested for a moment on the monkey-like hairs.

'False, obviously false,' he remarked with his lips, and I'm bound to confess I never saw any man speak so well by movement alone, you could follow every word, though not a sound escaped him.

During the rest of that evening, Dr. Hector MacPherson stuck to me as close as a mustard-plaster. And he was almost as irritating. I got heartily sick of the Upper Donside. I have positively waded in my time through ruby mines (in conversation, I mean) till the mere sight of a ruby absolutely sickens me. When Judas, in an unwonted fit of generosity, once gave his sister Mary (whom I had the honour to marry) a ruby necklet (inferior stones), I made Mary change it for sapphires and amethysts, on the judicious plea that they suited her complexion better. (I scored one, incidentally, for having considered Mary's complexion.) By the time I went to bed I was prepared to sink the Upper Donside in the sea, and to stab, strangle, poison, or otherwise seriously damage the man with the concession and the false eyebrows.

For the next three days, at intervals, he returned to the charge. He bored me to death with his platinum and his rubies. He didn't want a money lender who would personally exploit the thing, he would prefer to do it all on his own account, giving the money lender forty per cent. I listened and smiled, I listened and yawned, I listened and was rude, I ceased to listen at all, but still, he droned on with it. I fell asleep on a sail boat one day, and woke up in ten minutes to hear him droning yet: 'And the yield of platinum per ton was certified to be.' I forget how many shekels, or bekahs, or gerahs. Such details have ceased to interest me, like the man who 'didn't believe in ghosts,' I have seen too many of them.

The fresh-faced little rabbi and his wife however, were quite different people. He was an Aggadah expert from Issachar, she was a breezy Syrian lass, with a wholesome breath of the seas about her. I called her 'Supreme Crown' Their name was Brabazon. Camel traders are so accustomed to being beset by harpies of every description, that when they come across a young couple who are simple and natural, they delight in the purely human relation. We picnicked and went on excursions a great deal with the honeymooners. They were so frank in their young love, and so proof against chaff, that we all really liked them. But whenever I called the pretty girl 'Supreme Crown' she looked so shocked, and cried: 'Oh, Mr. Christ!' Still, we were the best of friends. The rabbi offered to row us in a boat on the lake one day, while the Syrian lassie assured us she could take an oar almost as well as he did. However, we did not accept their offer, as row-boats exert an unfavourable influence upon Martha's digestive organs.

'Nice young fellow, that man Brabazon,' Judas said to me one day, as we lounged together along the quay, 'never talks about Roman Emperors or becoming a Roman citizen. Doesn't seem to me to care two pins about promotion. Says he's quite content in his country synagogue, enough to live upon, and needs no more, and his wife has a little, a very little, money. I asked him about his poor today, on purpose to test him: these rabbis are always trying to screw something out of one for their poor, men in my position know the truth of the saying that we have that class of the population always with us. Would you believe it, he says he hasn't any poor at all in his parish! They're all well-to-do farmers or else able-bodied labourers, and his one terror is that somebody will come and try to pauperise them. 'If a philanthropist were to give me fifty minas today for use at Empingham,' he said, 'I assure you, Judas, I shouldn't know what to do with it. I think I should buy new dresses for Ellen, who wants them about as much as anybody else in the village - that is to say, not at all.' There's a rabbi for you, Jez, my boy. Only wish we had one of his sort at Bethlehem.'

'He certainly doesn't want to get anything out of you,' I answered.

That evening at dinner, a queer little episode happened. The man with the eyebrows began talking to me across the table in his usual fashion, full of his wearisome concession on the Upper Donside. I was trying to squash him as politely as possible, when I caught Martha's eye. Her look amused me. She was engaged in making signals to Judas at her side to observe the little rabbi's curious sleeve-links. I glanced at them, and saw at once they were a singular possession for so unobtrusive a person. They consisted each of a short gold bar for one arm of the link, fastened by a tiny chain of the same material to what appeared to my tolerably experienced eye as first-rate diamonds. Pretty big diamonds, too, and of remarkable shape, brilliancy, and cutting. In a moment, I knew what Martha meant. She owned a diamond riviere, said to be of Turkish origin, but short by two stones for the circumference of her tolerably ample neck.

Now, she had long been wanting two diamonds like these to match her set, but owing to the unusual shape and antiquated cutting of her own gems, she had never been able to complete the necklet, at least without removing an extravagant amount from a much larger stone of the first water.

The Syrian lassie's eyes caught Martha's at the same time, and she broke into a pretty smile of good-humoured amusement. 'Taken in another person, Isaac, dear!' she exclaimed, in her breezy way, turning to her husband. 'Lady Iscariot is observing your diamond sleeve-links.'

'They're very fine gems,' Martha observed, incautiously. (A most unwise admission, if she intended to buy them.)

But the pleasant little rabbi was too transparently simple a soul to take advantage of her slip of judgement. 'They are good stones,' he replied, 'very good stones, considering. They're not diamonds at all, to tell you the truth. They're best old-fashioned Oriental paste. My great-grandfather bought them, after the siege of Adapazarl, for a few leptons, from a Visigoth who had looted them from Hannibal's palace. He thought, like you, he had got a good thing. But it turned out, when they came to be examined by experts, they were only paste. Very wonderful paste. It is supposed they had even imposed upon Hannibal himself, so fine is the imitation. But they are worth - well, say, fifty drachmas at the utmost.'

While he spoke, Judas looked at Martha, and Martha looked at Judas. Their eyes spoke volumes. The riviere was also supposed to have come from Hannibals's collection. Both drew at once an identical conclusion. These were two of the same stones, very likely torn apart and disengaged from the rest in the melee at the capture of the Turkish palace.

'Can you take them off?' Judas asked, blandly. He spoke in the tone that indicates business.

'Certainly,' the little rabbi answered, smiling. 'I'm accustomed to taking them off. They're always noticed. They've been kept in the family ever since the siege, as a sort of valueless heirloom, for the sake of the picturesqueness of the story, you know, and nobody ever sees them without asking, as you do, to examine them closely. They deceive even experts at first. But they're paste, all the same, unmitigated Oriental paste, for all that.'

He took them both off, and handed them to Judas. No man in Judaea is a finer judge of gems than my brother-in-law. I watched him narrowly. He examined them close, first with the naked eye, then with the little pocket-lens which he always carries.

'Admirable imitation,' he muttered, passing them on to Martha. 'I'm not surprised they should impose upon inexperienced observers.'

But from the tone in which he said it, I could see at once he had satisfied himself they were real gems of unusual value. I know Judas's way of doing business so well. His glance to Martha meant, 'These are the very stones you have so long been in search of.'

The Syrian lassie laughed a merry laugh. 'He sees through them now, Isaac,' she cried. 'I felt sure Judas would be a judge of diamonds.'

Martha turned them over. I know Martha, too, and I knew from the way Martha looked at them that she meant to have them. And when Martha means to have anything, people who stand in the way may just as well spare themselves the trouble of opposing her.

They were beautiful diamonds. We found out afterwards the little rabbi's account was quite correct: these stones had come from the same necklet as Martha's riviere, made for a favourite wife of Hannibal's, who had presumably as expansive personal charms as our beloved sister-in-law's. More perfect diamonds have seldom been seen. They have excited the universal admiration of thieves and connoisseurs. Martha told me afterwards that, according to legend, a Visigoth stole the necklet at the sack of the palace, and then fought with another for it. It was believed that two stones got spilt in the scuffle, and were picked up and sold by a third person - a looker-on - who had no idea of the value of his booty. Martha had been hunting for them for several years, to complete her necklet.

'They are excellent paste,' Judas observed, handing them back. 'It takes a first-rate judge to detect them from the reality. Lady Iscariot has a necklet much the same in character, but composed of genuine stones, and as these are so much like them, and would complete her set, to all outer appearance, I wouldn't mind giving you, say, ten minas for the pair of them.'

Mrs. Brabazon looked delighted. 'Oh, sell them to him, Dick,' she cried, 'and buy me a brooch with the money! A pair of common links would do for you just as well. Ten minas for two paste stones! It's quite a lot of money.'

She said it so sweetly, with her pretty Syrian accent that I couldn't imagine how Isaac had the heart to refuse her. But he did, all the same.

'No, Ellen, darling,' he answered. 'They're worthless, I know, but they have for me a certain sentimental value, as I've often told you. My dear mother wore them, while she lived, as earrings, and as soon as she died, I had them set as links in order that I might always keep them about me. Besides, they have historical and family interest. Even a worthless heirloom, after all, is an heirloom.'

Dr. Hector MacPherson looked across and intervened. 'There is a part of my concession,' he said, 'where we have reason to believe a perfect new Eldorado will soon be discovered. If at any time you would care Judas, to look at my diamonds - when I get them - it would afford me the greatest pleasure in life to submit them to your consideration.'

Judas could stand it no longer. 'Sir,' he said, gazing across at him with his sternest air, 'if your concession were as full of diamonds as ageing whores are full of disease, I would not care to turn my head to look at them. I am acquainted with the nature and practice of salting.'

And he glared at the man with the overhanging eyebrows as if he would devour him raw. Poor Dr. Hector MacPherson subsided instantly. We learnt a little later that he was a harmless lunatic who went about the world with successive concessions for ruby mines and platinum reefs because he had been ruined and driven mad by speculations in the two, and now recouped himself by imaginary grants in Scotland and Estonia, or anywhere else that turned up handy. And his eyebrows, after all, were of Nature's handicraft. We were sorry for the incident, but a man in Judas's position is such a mark for rogues that, if he did not take means to protect himself promptly, he would be for ever overrun by them.

When we went up to our rooms that evening, Martha flung herself on the sofa. 'Judas,' she broke out in the voice of a drama queen, 'those are real diamonds, and I shall never be happy again till I get them.'

'They are real diamonds,' Judas echoed. 'And you shall have them, Martha. They're worth not less than three thousand minas. But I shall bid them up gently.'

So, next day, Judas set to work to haggle with the rabbi. Brabazon, however, didn't care to part with them. He was no money-grubber, he said. He cared more for his mother's gift and a family tradition than for a hundred minas, if Judas were to offer it. Judas's eye gleamed. 'But if I give you two hundred!' he said, insinuatingly. 'What opportunities for good! You could build a new wing to your village temple!'

'We have ample accommodation,' the rabbi answered. 'No, I don't think I'll sell them.'

Still, his voice faltered somewhat, and he looked down at them enquiringly.

Judas was too precipitate.

'A hundred minas more or less matters little to me,' he said, 'and my wife has set her heart on them. It's every man's duty to please his wife - isn't it, Mrs. Brabazon? - I offer you three hundred.'

The little Syrian girl clasped her hands.

'Three hundred minas! Oh, Isaac, just think what fun we could have, and what good we could do with it! Do let him have them.'

Her accent was irresistible. But the rabbi shook his head.

'Impossible,' he answered. 'My dear mother's earrings! Uncle Gobi would be so angry if he knew I'd sold them. I daren't face Uncle Gobi.'

'Has he expectations from Uncle Gobi?' Judas asked of

Supreme Crown.

Mrs. Brabazon laughed. 'Uncle Gobi! Oh, dear, no. Poor dear old Uncle Gobi! Why, the darling old soul hasn't a lepton to bless himself with, except his wine cellar. He's a retired vineyard worker.' And she laughed melodiously. She was a charming woman.

'Then I should disregard Uncle Gobi's feelings,' Judas said, decisively.

'No, no,' the rabbi answered. 'Poor dear old Uncle Gobi! I wouldn't do anything for the world to annoy him. And he'd be sure to notice it.'

We went back to Martha. 'Well, have you got them?' she asked.

'No,' Judas answered. 'Not yet. But he's coming round, I think. He's hesitating now. Would rather like to sell them himself, but is afraid what 'Uncle Gobi' would say about the matter. His wife will talk him out of his needless consideration for Uncle Gobi's feelings, and tomorrow we'll finally clench the bargain.'

Next morning we stayed late in our rooms, where we always breakfasted, and did not come down to the public bar till just before dinner, Judas being busy with me over arrears of correspondence. When we did come down, the inn keeper stepped forward with a twisted little feminine note for Martha. She took it and read it. Her countenance fell. 'There, Judas,' she cried, handing it to him, 'you've let the chance slip. I shall never be happy now! They've gone off with the diamonds.'

Judas seized the note and read it. Then he passed it on to me. It was short, but final:

'Thursday, 6 a.m. DEAR LADY ISCARIOT - Will you kindly excuse our having gone off hurriedly without bidding you goodbye? We have just had a horrid message to say that my husband's favourite sister is dangerously ill of fever in Rome. I wanted to shake hands with you before we left - you have all been so sweet to us - but we go by the morning camel train, absurdly early, and I wouldn't for the world disturb you. Perhaps some day we may meet again - though, buried as we are in a country village, it isn't likely, but in any case, you have secured the grateful recollection of yours very cordially, ELLEN BRABAZON. P.S. Kindest regards to Judas and those dear Christs, and a kiss for yourself, if I may venture to send you one.'

'She doesn't even mention where they've gone,' Martha exclaimed, in a very bad humour.

'The inn keeper may know,' Mary suggested, looking over my shoulder.

We asked at his office.

Yes, the gentleman's address was the Rabbi Isaac Adam Brabazon, Holme Bush Cottage, Empingham, Galilee.

Any address where letters might be sent at once, in Rome? For the next ten days, or till further notice, Inn Della Apollo, Via Caesar Battisti.

Martha's mind was made up at once: 'Strike while the iron's hot,' she cried. 'This sudden illness, coming at the end of their honeymoon, and involving ten days' more stay at an expensive inn, will probably upset the rabbi's budget. He'll be glad to sell now. You'll get them for three hundred. It was absurd of Judas to offer so much at first, but offered once, of course we must stick to it.'

'What do you propose to do?' Judas asked. 'Write, or send a messenger?'

'Oh, how silly men are!' Martha cried. 'Is this the sort of business to be arranged by letter, still less by messenger? No. Jesus must start off at once, taking tonight's camel train, and the moment he gets to Rome, he must interview the rabbi or Mrs. Brabazon. Mrs. Brabazon's the best. She has none of this stupid, sentimental nonsense about Uncle Gobi.'

It is no part of a secretary's duties to act as a diamond broker. But when Martha puts her foot down, she puts her foot down - a fact which she is unnecessarily fond of emphasising in that identical proposition. So the self-same evening saw me safe in the camel train on my way to Rome, and four days later I alighted from a ship at the main Roman quay. My orders were to bring back those diamonds, dead or alive so to speak, in my pocket, to Amman, and to offer any needful sum, up to two thousand five hundred minas, for their immediate purchase.

When I arrived at the Della Apollo I found the poor little rabbi and his wife both greatly agitated. They had sat up all night, they said, with their invalid sister and the sleeplessness and suspense had certainly told upon them after their long journey. They were pale and tired, Mrs. Brabazon in particular looking ill and worried. I was more than half ashamed of bothering them about the diamonds at such a moment, but it occurred to me that Martha was probably right, they would now have reached the end of the sum set apart for their jaunt, and a little ready cash might be far from unwelcome.

I broached the subject delicately. It was a fad of lady Iscariot's, I said. She had set her heart upon those useless trinkets. And she wouldn't go without them. She must and would have them. But the rabbi was obdurate. He threw Uncle Gobi still in my teeth. Three hundred? No, never! A mother's present, impossible, dear Ellen! Ellen begged and prayed, she had grown really attached to Lady Iscariot, she said, but the rabbi wouldn't hear of it. I went up tentatively to four hundred. He shook his head gloomily. It wasn't a question of money, he said. It was a question of affection. I saw it was no use trying that tack any longer. I struck out a new line. 'These stones,' I said, 'I think I ought to inform you, are really diamonds. Judas is certain of it. Now, is it right for a man of your profession and position to be wearing a pair of big gems like those, worth several hundred minas, as ordinary sleeve-links? A woman? Yes, I grant you, but for a man, is it manly? And you a kabalist!'

He looked at me and laughed. 'Will nothing convince you?' he cried. 'They have been examined and tested by half-a-dozen jewellers, and we know them to be paste. It wouldn't be right of me to sell them to you under false pretences, however unwilling on my side. I couldn't do it.'

'Well, then,' I said, going up a bit in my bids to meet him, 'I'll put it like this. These gems are paste. But Lady Iscariot has an unconquerable and unaccountable desire to possess them. Money doesn't matter to her. She is a friend of your wife's. As a personal favour, won't you sell them to her for a thousand?'

He shook his head. 'It would be wrong,' he said, 'I might even add, criminal.'

'But we take all risk,' I cried.

He was absolute adamant. 'As a rabbi,' he answered, 'I feel I cannot do it.'

'Will you try, Mrs. Brabazon?' I asked.

The pretty little Syrian leant over and whispered. She coaxed and cajoled him. Her ways were winsome. I couldn't hear what she said, but he seemed to give way at last. 'I should love Lady Iscariot to have them,' she murmured, turning to me. 'She is such a dear!' And she took out the links from her husbands cuffs and handed them across to me.

'How much?' I asked.

'Two thousand?' she answered interrogatively. It was a big rise all at once, but such are the ways of women.

'Done!' I replied. 'Do you consent?'

The rabbi looked up as if ashamed of himself.

'I consent,' he said, slowly, 'since Ellen wishes it. But as a rabbi, and to prevent any future misunderstanding, I should like you to give me a statement in writing that you buy them on my distinct and positive declaration that they are made of paste - old Oriental paste - not genuine stones, and that I do not claim any other qualities for them.'

I popped the gems into my purse, well pleased.

'Certainly,' I said, pulling out a paper. Judas, with his unerring business instinct, had anticipated the request, and given me a signed agreement to that effect.

'You will take a credit note payable by a reputable money lender?' I inquired.

He hesitated. 'Gold coins would suit me better, aureus,'

he answered.

'Very well,' I replied. ' I will go out and get them.'

How very unsuspicious some people are! He allowed me go off with the stones in my pocket!

Judas had given me a blank credit note, not exceeding two thousand five hundred minas. I took it to a money lender and cashed it for gold coins. The rabbi clasped a handful of them with pleasure, there were too many to hold with ease in his hands. And right glad I was to go back to Amman that night, feeling that I had got those diamonds into my hands for about a thousand minas under their real value!

At Amman camel station Martha met me. She was positively agitated.

'Have you bought them, Jesus?' she asked.

'Yes,' I answered, producing my spoils in triumph.

'Oh, how dreadful!' she cried, drawing back. 'Do you think they're real? Are you sure he hasn't cheated you?'

'Certain of it,' I replied, examining them. 'No one can take me in, in the matter of diamonds. Why on earth should you doubt them?'

'Because I've been talking to the cook at the inn, and she says there's a well-known trick just like that. A swindler has two sets, one real, one false, and he makes you buy the false ones by showing you the real, and pretending he sells them as a special favour.'

'You needn't be alarmed,' I answered. 'I am a judge of diamonds.'

'I shan't be satisfied,' Martha murmured, 'till Judas has seen them.'

We went up to the inn. For the first time in her life I saw Martha really nervous as I handed the stones to Judas to examine. Her doubt was contagious. I half feared, myself, he might break out into a deep monosyllabic interjection, losing his temper in haste, as he often does when things go wrong. But he looked at them with a smile, while I told him the price.

'Eight hundred minas less than their value,' he

answered, well satisfied.

'You have no doubt of their reality?' I asked.

'Not the slightest,' he replied, gazing at them. 'They are genuine stones, precisely the same in quality and type as Martha's necklet.'

Martha drew a sigh of relief. 'I'll go upstairs,' she said, slowly, 'and bring down my own for you both to compare with them.'

One minute later, she rushed down again, breathless. Martha is far from slim, and I never before knew her exert herself so actively.

'Judas, Judas!' she cried, 'do you know what dreadful thing has happened? Two of my own stones are gone. He's stolen a couple of diamonds from my necklet, and sold them back to me.'

She held out the riviere. It was all too true. Two gems were missing, and these two just fitted the empty places!

A light broke in upon me. I clapped my hand to my head. 'By Moses,' I exclaimed, 'the little rabbi is Arugath ha-Bosem!'

Judas clapped his own hand to his brow in turn. 'And Ellen,' he cried, 'Supreme Crown that innocent little Syrian! I often detected a familiar ring in her voice, in spite of the charming accent. Ellen is Madame Picardet!'

We had absolutely no evidence, but, like the Commissary at Naples, we felt instinctively sure of it.

Judas was determined to catch the rogue. This second deception put him on his mettle. 'The worst of the man is,' he said, 'he has a method. He doesn't go out of his way to cheat us, he makes us go out of ours to be cheated. He lays a trap, and we tumble headlong into it. Tomorrow, Jez, we must follow him on to Rome.'

Martha explained to him what the cook had said. Judas took it all in at once, with his usual sagacity. 'That explains,' he said, 'why the rascal used this particular trick to draw us on by. If we had suspected him, he could have shown the diamonds were real, and so escaped detection. It was a blind to draw us off from the fact of the robbery. He went to Rome to be out of the way when the discovery was made, and to get a clear start on us. What a consummate rogue! And to do me twice running!'

'How did he get at my jewel-case, though?' Martha exclaimed.

'That's the question,' Judas answered. 'You do leave it about so!'

'And why didn't he steal the whole riviere at once, and sell the gems?' I inquired.

'Too cunning,' Judas replied. 'This was much better business. It isn't easy to dispose of a big thing like that. In the first place, the stones are large and valuable. In the second place, they're well known, every dealer has heard of the Iscariot riviere and seen drawings of the shape of them. They're marked gems, so to speak. No, he played a better game. Took a couple of them off and offered them to the only person on earth who was likely to buy them without suspicion. He came here meaning to work this very trick. He had the links made right to the shape beforehand, then stole the stones and slipped them into their places. It's a wonderfully clever trick. Upon my soul, I almost admire the fellow.'

For Judas is a trader himself, and can appreciate sales tricks in others.

We followed Arugath ha-Bosem on to Rome. It was all in vain. The rabbi and his wife, we found, quitted the Inn Della Apollo for parts unknown that same afternoon. And, as usual with Arugath ha-Bosem, they vanished into space, leaving no clue behind them. In other words, they changed their disguise, no doubt, and reappeared somewhere else that night in altered characters. At any rate, no such person as the Rabbi Isaac Adam Brabazon was ever afterwards heard of and no such village exists as Empingham, Galilee.

We communicated the matter to the Roman police. They were most unsympathetic. 'It is no doubt Arugath ha-Bosem,' said the official whom we saw, 'but you seem to have little just ground of complaint against him. As far as I can see, messieurs, there is not much to choose between you. You, Mister Blockhead, deed to buy diamonds at the price of paste. You, missus, feared you had bought paste at the price of diamonds. You, master the secretary, tried to get the stones from an unsuspecting person for half their value. He took you all in, that brave Arugath Caoutchouc, it was diamond cut diamond.'

Which was true, no doubt, but by no means consoling.

We returned to the Grand Inn. Judas was fuming with indignation. 'This is really too much,' he exclaimed. 'What an audacious rascal! But he will never again take me in, my dear Jez. I only hope he'll try it on. I should love to catch him. I'd know him another time, I'm sure, in spite of his disguises. It's absurd my being tricked twice running like this. But never again while I live! Never again, I declare to you!'

'This one beats a rat!' a courier in the hall close by murmured responsively. We stood under the veranda of the Grand Inn, in the big glass courtyard. And I verily believed that the courier was really Arugath ha-Bosem himself in one of his disguises. But perhaps we were beginning to suspect him everywhere.

CHAPTER FOUR

Shortly after the incidents just related, Arugath ha-Bosem knowing my weakness for the fairer sex, played a trick on me. A note led me to a room where I believed I would enjoy the sex slave of a merchant who wished to do business with Judas Iscariot and thought I might petition his case. Or at least this is what Arugath ha-Bosem led me to believe. I eyed up the concubine and she was a meek-eyed, timid-looking thing. However, merely for thrusting my hands into her breasts she flew at me like a tiger, and my face was instantly furrowed by her cursed nails like unto a field new ploughed. When somewhat recovered from the surprise occasioned by her sudden attack, I hired some eunuchs with my master's money and delivered the termagant into their care.

In a few days my face was well, my instructions that the slave responsible for the attack should be treated with every possible respect had put her off her guard. One morning when Judas was at the bazaar, I had the eunuchs convey her into his sex chamber, where before she could tell what they were about, her hands were securely fastened together and drawn above her head, through a pulley fixed in the ceiling. I directed her to be pulled up so as not to lift her off the ground, but that she should not be able to throw herself down. When this was effected I entered the room and dismissed the eunuchs. There she stood trembling with rage, but unable to help herself. I now drew a couch towards her, and having seated myself close to her, placed one arm around her waist, and with the other attempted to lift up her robes.

It is impossible to describe the exertions she made to prevent my proceedings, she twisted herself about and writhed and kicked until I was obliged to abandon my attempt for a moment and call in the eunuchs, who quickly (in spite of her kicking) secured each of her feet to a ring placed in the floor, set slightly under two cubits apart from each other. This, of course, considerably extended her legs and thighs. She was then secure in every way. After dismissing the eunuchs, I again drew the couch close to her, and without further ceremony lifted up her robe. What delicious transports shot through my veins at the voluptuous charms exhibited to my ardent gaze. How lovely was her round mount of love, just above the temple of Venus, superbly covered with beautiful black hair, how soft and smooth as ivory her belly and her swelling, delicately formed thighs.

The cygnet down instantly disclosed that she was a maid, for where two bodies have been properly joined in the fierce encounter, the hair (particularly of the female) loses that sleek downy appearance, and by the constant friction smooth hair becomes rubbed into delightful little curls. But, to put the fact beyond dispute, I thrust my forefinger into the little hole below. Her loud cries and the difficulty of entering which was found, set the fact beyond dispute. Immediately dropping on my knees, grasping in each hand one of her buttocks, I placed on her virgin toy a most delicious kiss. I then got up and began to undress her. She appeared nearly choked with passion, her tears flowed down her beautiful face in torrents. But her rage was of no use. Proceeding leisurely, first unwrapping one thing, then another, and with the help of a knife, I quickly rid her of her covering.

What a glorious sight she exhibited: beautiful breasts - finely placed, sufficiently firm to support themselves - shoulders, belly, thighs, legs, everything was deliciously voluptuous. But what most struck my fancy was the beautiful whiteness, roundness and voluptuous swell of the firm flesh of her lovely buttocks and thighs. 'Soon,' I said to myself, handling her delicious backside, 'soon shall this lovely whiteness be mixed with a crimson blush.' I placed burning kisses upon every part of her, wherever my lips travelled instantly the part was covered with scarlet blushes. Having directed two rods to be placed on the couch, also a leather whip with broad lashes, I took one of the rods (shoving the couch out of the way) and began gently to lay it on the beautiful posterior of my sobbing captive. At first I did it gently enough - it could have no other effect than just to tickle her, but shortly I began every now and then to lay on a smart lash, which made her wince and cry out.

This tickling and cutting I kept up for some time - until the alabaster cheeks of her arse had become suffused with a slight blush - then suddenly I began to give the rod with all my might, then indeed was every lash followed by a cry, or an exclamation of pity. Her winces and the delicious wiggling of her backside increased in proportion to the intensity of my blows and these continued, heedless of her entreaties. When I stopped, the entire surface of her buttocks was covered with welts, every here and there, where the stem of the leaves had caught her, appeared a little spot of crimson blood, which went trickling down the lily thighs. Again and again did I slide my hand over her numerous beauties. Again and again did my forefinger intrude itself into her delicate little hole of pleasure. She could not avoid anything I thought fit to do. Her thighs were stretched wide enough for me to have enjoyed her if I had thought fit, but that was not my immediate intention. I had decided she was to receive more punishment before she was deflowered.

I stripped myself, and seizing the leather whip, began to flog her with such effect that blood flowed with every lash. Vain were her cries and supplications - still lash followed lash in rapid succession. I was now in so princely a state of erection that I could have made a hole where there had been none before, let alone drive myself into a place which nature had been so bountiful as to form of stretching material. Quickly summoning the eunuchs, I directed them to lay her on her back of the couch, properly securing an arm on each side to one of the legs of the couch. It was accomplished almost as quickly as ordered. The eunuchs retired, leaving me with my exhausted victim to complete the sacrifice. I was not long in rooting up her modesty, deprived as she was of the use of her arms and exhausted by her sufferings. A pillow had been placed under her sufficiently to raise her bottom so as to leave a fair mark for my engine, I threw her legs over my shoulders, and softly (as a tender mother playing with her infant) opened the lips of paradise and love to reveal its coral hue and mossy little grotto - and each fold closed upon the intruding finger, repelling the unwelcome guest.

Inconceivable is the delight one feels in these transporting situations. There is nothing on earth so much enhances the stimulation for with me as to know the object that affords me the pleasure detests me - her tears and looks of anguish are sources of unutterable joy to me. Being satisfied in every way, by sight, by touch, by every sense, that I was the first possessor, I placed the head of my instrument between the distended lips, grasping her thighs with her legs over my shoulders, then making a formidable thrust, lodged the head entirely in her, she turned her beautiful eyes up to heaven as if looking there for assistance - her exhaustion precluded any opposition, another fierce thrust deepened the insertion, tears in torrents followed my efforts, but she disdained to speak, still I thrust, but no complaint, but growing fiercer, one formidable plunge proved too mighty for her forbearance - she not only screamed, but struggled. However, I was safely in her. Another thrust finished the job, it was done, and nobly done.

After having cooled my burning passion by copious discharge, I withdrew myself. Crimson tears followed my exit, with a handkerchief I wiped away the precious drops and falling on my knees between her thighs, placed on the torn and wounded lips a delicious kiss - delicious beyond measure. Only consider that no one but myself had divided these pouting, fresh, warm, clasping and gaping gates of pleasure. Indeed it was beyond description. I now thought it time to untie the silken cord that confined the arms of this young vixen. On feeling her arms released, her only motion was to cover her eyes with her hands, there she lay on her back immovable - but for her sobs. I could not have told whether she existed. I left her, but ordered the eunuchs to convey her to her prison where they were to take the greatest care of her.

CHAPTER FIVE

Like most camel traders, Judas Iscariot is anything but sedentary. He hates sitting down. He must always 'trek.' He cannot live without moving about freely. Six weeks in Bethlehem at a time is as much as he can stand. Then he must run away incontinently for rest and change to Syria, Turkey, Palermo, Jerusalem. 'I won't be a limpet on the rock,' he says. Thus it came to pass that in the early autumn we found ourselves stopping at The Talk Of The Town Inn on the Persian Bay in Babylon. We were the accustomed nice little family party. Judas and Martha, myself and Mary, with the suite as usual.

On the first Saturday morning after our arrival we strolled out, Judas and I - I regret to say during the hours allotted for Divine service - on to the King's Road, to get a whiff of fresh air, and a glimpse of the waves that were churning the channel. The two ladies (with their bonnets) had gone to synagogue, but Judas had risen late, fatigued from the week's toil, while I myself was suffering from a headache, which I attributed to the close air in the dice-room overnight, combined, perhaps, with the insidious effect of a brand of sweet-wine to which I was little accustomed, I had used it to dull my senses and thus level the playing field, since when sober I was a greatly superior dice-man to anyone present. We were to meet our wives afterwards at the synagogue parade, an institution to which I believe both Martha and Mary attach even greater importance than to the sermon which precedes it.

We sat down on a glass seat. Judas gazed enquiringly up and down the King's Road, on the look-out for a boy with Saturday sweet bread . At last one passed. 'chola' ' my brother-in-law called out laconically.

'Ain't got none,' the boy answered, brandishing his wares in our faces. ''Ave some bagels, some platzels or some black bread?'

Judas, however, eats black bread all week, while as to

the bagels or platzels, he simply prefers a loaf and on Saturday morning that meant chola. So he shook his head, and muttered, 'If you pass someone selling sweet white loaves, send him on here at once to me.'

A polite stranger who sat close to us turned round with a pleasant smile. 'Would you allow me to offer you a slice?' he said, drawing platted chola from a bag and cutting it with a knife he withdrew from a pocket. 'I fancy I bought the last. There's a run on them today, you see. People are fortifying themselves against the news from Phoenicia.'

Judas raised his eyebrows, and accepted the slice which he hurriedly buttered, as I thought, just a trifle grumpily. So, to remove the false impression his surliness might produce on so benevolent a mind, I entered into conversation with the polite stranger. He was a man of middle age and medium height, with a cultivated air. His eyes were sharp, his voice was refined, he dropped into talk before long about distinguished people just then in Babylon. It was clear at once that he was hand in glove with many of the very best kind. We compared notes as to Naples, Rome, Florence, Cairo. Our new acquaintance had scores of friends in common with us, it seemed, indeed, our circles so largely coincided, that I wondered we had never happened till then to knock up against one another.

'And Judas Iscariot, the great camel trader,' he said at last, 'do you know anything of him? I'm told he's at present down here at The Talk Of The Town Inn.'

I waved my hand towards the person in question.

'This is Judas Iscariot,' I answered, with proprietary pride, 'and I am his brother-in-law, Mr. Jesus H. Christ.'

'Oh, indeed!' the stranger answered, with a curious air of drawing in his horns. I wondered whether he had just been going to pretend he knew Judas, or whether perchance he was on the point of saying something highly uncomplimentary, and was glad to have escaped it.

By this time, however, Judas had wolfed down his slice and chimed into our conversation. I could see at once from his mollified tone that the chola had taken the edge off his hunger, which was all that had bothered him, since while the news from Phoenicia was considered a disaster by many, it was favourable to our operations as camel dealers. Judas was therefore in a friendly and affable temper. His whole manner changed at once. He grew polite in return to the polite stranger. Besides, we knew the man moved in the best society, he had acquaintances whom Martha was most anxious to secure for her at homes in Bezethar - including several Roman senators and Solomon ibn Adreth, the famous time traveller. As for the kabalists, it was clear that he was sworn friends with the whole lot of them. He dined with the masters of this art, and gave weekly breakfasts for their students. Now, Martha is particularly desirous that her salon should not be considered too exclusively secular in character with a solid basis of traders, she loves a delicate under-current of literature, art, and the religious classes.

Our new acquaintance was extremely communicative: 'Knows his place in society, Jez,' Judas said to me afterwards, 'and is therefore not afraid of talking freely, as so many people are who have doubts about their position.' We exchanged cards before we rose. Our new friend's name turned out to be Dr. Jacob Ben Shesheth.

'Do you have a cure for clap?' I inquired, though his garb belied it.

'Oh, no I don't practice magick publicly,' he answered. 'I am a speculative kabalist. don't you know. I interest myself in religious icons, and buy to some extent for the Temple in Jerusalem.'

'The very man for Martha's at homes!' Judas snapped at him instantly. 'I've brought several camels down here with me,' he said, in his best friendly manner, 'and we are thinking of tooling over tomorrow to the hanging gardens. If you'd care to take a seat beside a hump I'm sure Lady Iscariot would be charmed to see you.'

'You're very kind,' the kabalist said, 'on so casual an introduction. I'm sure I shall be delighted.'

'We start from The Talk Of The Town Inn at ten-thirty,' Judas went on.

'I shall be there. Good morning!' And, with a satisfied smile, he rose and left us, nodding.

We returned to the sea, to Martha and Mary.

Our new friend passed us once or twice. Judas stopped him and introduced him. He was walking with two ladies, most elegantly dressed in rather peculiar brightly coloured robes. Martha was taken at first sight by his manner. 'One could see at a glance,' she said, 'he was a person of culture and of real distinction. I wonder whether he could bring some kabalists to my salon on Wednesday fortnight?'

Next day, at ten-thirty, we started on our ride. Our camels were considered the best in Babylon. Judas is an excellent, though somewhat anxious - or, might I say better, somewhat careful - whip. He finds the management of the leading camel fills his hands for the moment, both literally and figuratively, leaving very little time for general conversation. Lady Belleisle rode behind him, Dr. Ben Shesheth occupied the camel just behind with myself and Martha just behind him. The kabalist talked most of the time to Lady Iscariot: his discourse was of religious icons which Martha detests, but in which she thinks it incumbent upon her, as Judas's wife, to affect now and then a cultivated interest. Noblesse oblige, and the walls of our place in Bethlehem are almost covered now with craven images.

Dr. Ben Shesheth, in spite of his too pronouncedly religious talk, proved on closer view a most agreeable companion. He diversified his art cleverly with anecdotes and scandals, he told us exactly which famous kabalists had married their cooks, and which had only married their student's sisters, and otherwise showed himself a most diverting talker. Among other things, however, he happened to mention once that he had recently discovered a genuine tablet brought down by Moses from the mountain - a quite undoubted Holy tablet of stone, which had remained for years in the keeping of a certain obscure Roman family. It had always been allowed to be the very thing that Moses had got from God, but it had seldom been seen for the last half-century save by a few intimate acquaintances.

I saw Judas prick up his ears, though he took no open notice. The famous Moses, as it happened, was a remote collateral ancestor of the Iscariots, and the existence of the tablet of stone, though not its whereabouts, was well known in the family. Mary had often mentioned it. If it was to be had at anything like a reasonable price, it would be a splendid thing for the boys (Judas, I ought to say, has two sons studying at the Temple in Jerusalem) to possess an undoubted tablet that had been brought down from the mountain by Moses.

Dr. Ben Shesheth talked a good deal after that about this valuable find. He had tried to sell it at first to the Temple, but though the priests admired the stone carvings on it immensely, and admitted its genuineness, they regretted that the funds at their disposal this year did not permit them to acquire so important a piece of stone at a proper figure. The Essenes again were too poor, but the kabalist was in treaty at present with some Greeks and with the Emperor. Still, it was a pity a fine piece of Judaic heritage like that, once brought into the hands of the faith, should be allowed to go out of it. Some patriotic follower of Judaic law ought to buy it for his own house, or else munificently present it to the faith.

All the time Judas said nothing. But I could feel him cogitating. He even looked behind him once, near a difficult sand dune, and gave Martha a warning glance to say nothing committing, which had at once the requisite effect of sealing her mouth for the moment. It is a very unusual thing for Judas to look back while leading a camel train. I gathered from his doing so that he was inordinately anxious to possess this tablet of stone.

When we arrived at the hanging gardens we put up our camels at the inn, and Judas ordered a lunch on his wonted scale of princely magnificence. Meanwhile we wandered, two and two, about the horticultural wonder. I annexed Lady Belleisle, who is at least amusing. Judas drew me aside before starting.

'Look here, Jez,' he said, 'we must be very careful. This man, Ben Shesheth, is a chance acquaintance. There's nothing over which an astute rogue can take one in more easily than an old religious relic. If the tablet of stone is genuine I ought to have it. I owe it to the boys to buy it. But I've been done twice lately, and I won't be done a third time. We must go to work cautiously.'

'You are right,' I answered. 'No more seers and rabbis!'

'If this man's an impostor,' Judas went on, 'and in spite of what he says about the Temple at Jerusalem and so forth, we know nothing of him, the story he tells is just the sort of one such a fellow would trump up in a moment to deceive me. He could easily learn who I was. I'm a well-known figure, he knew I was in Babylon, and he may have been sitting on that glass seat on Saturday on purpose to entrap me.'

'He introduced your name,' I said, 'and the moment he found out who I was he plunged into talk with me.'

'Yes,' Judas continued. 'He may have learned about the tablet of stone, which my grandmother always said was preserved at Gouda, and, indeed, I myself have often mentioned it, as you doubtless remember. If so, what more natural, say, for a rogue than to begin talking about the tablet of stone in that innocent way to Martha? If he wants a tablet of stone, I believe they can be turned out to order to any amount in Gaul. The moral of all this is, it behoves us to be careful.'

'Right you are,' I answered, 'and I am keeping my eye upon him.'

We drove back by another route, which offered the opportunity of a picnic at an oasis. It was a delightful excursion. Dr. Ben Shesheth's heart was elated by lunch and the excellent red wine. He talked amazingly. I never heard a man with a greater or more varied flow of anecdote. He had been everywhere and knew all about everybody. Martha booked him at once for her salon on Wednesday week, and he promised to introduce her to several rabbinical and kabalistic celebrities.

That evening, however, about half-past seven, Judas and I strolled out together on the King's Road for a blow before dinner. We dine at eight. The air was delicious. We passed a small new inn, very smart and exclusive, with a big bow window. There, in evening robes, lights burning and blind up, sat our friend, Dr. Ben Shesheth, with a lady facing him, young, graceful, and pretty. A flagon of wine stood between them. He was helping himself plentifully to grapes, and was full of good humour. It was clear he and the lady were occupied in the intense enjoyment of some capital joke, for they looked queerly at one another, and burst now and again into merry peals of laughter.

I drew back. So did Judas. One idea passed at once through both our minds. I murmured, 'Arugath ha-Bosem!' He answered, 'And Madame Picardet!'

They were not in the least like the Rabbi Isaac and Mrs. Brabazon. But that clinched the matter. Nor did I see a sign of the aquiline nose of the Druid Seer. Still, I had learnt by then to discount appearances. If this was indeed the famous sharper and his wife or accomplice, we must be very careful. We were forewarned this time. Supposing he had the audacity to try a third trick upon us we had him under our thumbs. Only, we must take steps to prevent his dexterously slipping through our fingers.

'He can wriggle like an eel,' said the Commissary at Naples. We both recalled those words, and laid our plans deep to prevent the man's wriggling away from us on this third occasion.

'I tell you what it is, Jez,' my brother-in-law said, with impressive slowness. 'This time we must deliberately lay ourselves out to be swindled. We must propose of our own accord to buy the tablet of stone, making him guarantee it in writing as a genuine relic passed down from Moses, and taking care to tie him down by most stringent conditions. But we must seem at the same time to be unsuspicious and innocent as babes. We must swallow whole whatever lies he tells us. Pay his price, nominally, by credit note for the stone. Then arrest him the moment the bargain is complete, with the proofs of his guilt there upon him. Of course, what he'll try to do will be to vanish into thin air at once, as he did at Naples and Rome, but, this time, we'll have the police in waiting and everything ready. We'll avoid precipitancy, but we'll avoid delay too. We must hold our hands off till he's actually accepted and pocketed the money, and then, we must nab him instantly, and walk him off to the local goal. That's my plan of campaign. Meanwhile, we should appear all trustful innocence and confiding guilelessness.'

In pursuance of this well-laid scheme, we called next day on Dr. Ben Shesheth at his inn, and were introduced to his wife, a dainty little woman, in whom we affected not to recognise that arch Madame Picardet or that simple Supreme Crown. The kabalist talked charmingly (as usual) about his art, what a well-informed rascal he was, and Judas expressed some interest in the supposed tablet of stone. Our new friend was delighted, we could see by his well-suppressed eagerness of tone that he knew us at once for probable purchasers. He would run across country next day, he said, and bring down the tablet. And in effect, when Judas and I took our wonted places in the camel train next morning, on our way up to the half-yearly meeting with our most important trading partners, there was our kabalist, sitting astride a camel as if every beast in the train belonged to him. Judas gave me an expressive look. 'Does it in style,' he whispered, 'doesn't he? Takes it out of my five thousand, or discounts the amount he means to cheat me of with his spurious tablet.'

Arriving in town, we went to work at once. We set a private detective recently retired from the Praetorian Guard to watch our friend, and from him we learned that the so-called kabalist dropped in for a curved stone tablet that day at a trader's in the bazaar, a trader who was known to be mixed up before then in several shady or disreputable transactions. Though, to be sure, my experience has been that religious relic dealers are religious relic dealers. Camels rank first in my mind as begetters and producers of unscrupulous agents, but religious relics run them a very good second. Anyhow, we found out that our distinguished kabalist picked up his stone tablet at this dealer's stall, and left again the same night for Babylon.

In order not to act precipitately, and so ruin our plans, we induced Dr. Ben Shesheth (what a cleverly chosen name!) to bring the tablet of stone round to The Talk Of The Town Inn for our inspection, and to leave it with us while we got the opinion of an expert from Bethlehem.

The expert came down, and gave us a full report upon the alleged relic. In his judgement, it was not the tablet Moses had brought down from the mountain at all, but a poorly-carved and well-begrimed modern Gaulish imitation. Moreover, he showed us by documentary evidence that the real tablet had, as a matter of fact, been taken to Rome five years before, and sold to a senator, a well-known connoisseur of antiquities, for eight thousand minas. Dr. Ben Shesheth's stone was, therefore, a mere modern forgery.

We were thus well prepared to fasten our charge of criminal conspiracy upon the self-styled kabalist. But in order to make assurance still more certain, we threw out vague hints to him that the genuine stone tablet might really be elsewhere, and even suggested in his hearing that it might not improbably have got into the hands of that omnivorous collector in Rome. But the vendor was proof against all such attempts to decry his goods. He had the effrontery to brush away the documentary evidence, and to declare the Roman senator (one of the most learned and astute antiquarians in the Empire) had been smartly imposed upon by a needy Gaulish con-artist with a talent for forgery. The real stone tablet, he declared and swore, was the one he offered us. 'Success has turned the man's head,' Judas said to me, well pleased. 'He thinks we will swallow any obvious lie he chooses to palm off upon us. But the bucket has come once too often to the well. This time we checkmate him.' It was a mixed metaphor, I admit, but Judas's tropes are not always entirely superior to criticism.

So we pretended to believe our man, and accepted his assurances. Next came the question of price. This was warmly debated, for form's sake only. The Roman senator had paid eight thousand for his genuine stone tablet. The kabalist demanded ten thousand for his spurious one. There was really no reason why we should haggle and dispute, for Judas meant merely to give his credit note for the sum and then arrest the fellow, but, still, we thought it best for the avoidance of suspicion to make a show of resistance, and we at last beat him down to nine thousand talents. For this amount he was to give us a written warranty that the work he sold us was a genuine stone tablet brought down by Moses from the mountain, that it represented the words of God, and that he had bought it himself, without doubt or question, from a direct descendent of Moses living at Gouda.

It was capitally done. We arranged the thing to perfection. We had a constable in waiting in our rooms at The Talk Of The Town Inn, and we settled that Dr. Ben Shesheth was to call at the inn at a certain fixed hour to sign the warranty and receive his money. A regular agreement on sound stamped papyrus was drawn out between us. At the appointed time the 'party of the first part' came, having already given us over possession of the tablet. Judas drew a credit note for the amount agreed upon, and signed it. Then he handed it to the kabalist. Ben Shesheth just clutched at it. Meanwhile, I took up my post by the door, while two men in plain togas, detectives from the Babylonian police-force, stood as men-servants and watched the windows. We feared lest the impostor, once he had got the cheque, should dodge us somehow, as he had already done at Naples and in Rome. The moment he had pocketed his money with a smile of triumph, I advanced to him rapidly. I had in my possession a stiff rope to bind him with. Before he knew what was happening, I had slipped the string around his wrists and secured his arms dexterously behind his back, while the constable stepped forward. 'We have got you this time!' I cried. 'We know who you are, Dr. Ben Shesheth. You are Arugath ha-Bosem, alias Laird Archibald McArchibald, alias the Rabbi Isaac Adam Brabazon.'

I never saw any man so astonished in my life! He was utterly flabbergasted. Judas thought he must have expected to get clear away at once, and that this prompt action on our part had taken the fellow so much by surprise as to simply unman him. He gazed about him as if he hardly realised what was happening.

'Are these two raving maniacs?' he asked at last, 'or what do they mean by this nonsensical gibberish about Laird Archibald McArchibald?'

The constable laid his hand on the prisoner's shoulder.

'It's all right, my man,' he said. 'We've got warrants out against you. I arrest you, Jacob Ben Shesheth, alias Rabbi Isaac Adam Brabazon, on a charge of obtaining money under false pretences from Judas Iscariot, on his sworn information, now here subscribed to.' For Judas had the thing drawn out in readiness beforehand.

Our prisoner drew himself up. 'Look here, officer,' he said, in an offended tone, 'there's some mistake here in this matter. I have never given an alias at any time in my life. How do you know this is really Judas Iscariot? It may be a case of bullying impersonation. My belief is, though, they're a pair of escaped lunatics.'

'We'll see about that tomorrow,' the constable said, collaring him. 'At present you've got to go off with me quietly to the goal, where these gentlemen will enter up the charge against you.'

They carried him off, protesting. Judas and I signed the charge-sheet, and the officer locked him up to await his examination next day before the magistrate.

We were half afraid even then the fellow would manage somehow to get out on bail and give us the slip in spite of everything, and, indeed, he protested in the most violent manner against the treatment to which we were subjecting 'a gentleman in his position.' But Judas took care to tell the police it was all right, that he was a dangerous and peculiarly slippery criminal, and that on no account must they let him go on any pretext whatever, till he had been properly examined before the magistrates.

We learned at the inn that night, curiously enough, that there really is a Dr. Ben Shesheth, a distinguished kabalist, whose name, we didn't doubt, our impostor had been assuming.

Next morning, when we reached the court, an inspector met us with a very long face. 'Look here, gentlemen,' he said, 'I'm afraid you've committed a very serious blunder. You've made a precious bad mess of it. You've got yourselves into a scrape, and, what's worse, you've got us into one also. You were a deal too smart with your sworn information. We've made inquiries about this gentleman, and we find the account he gives of himself is perfectly correct. His name is Ben Shesheth, he's a well-known kabalist and collector of religious relics and icons, employed abroad by the Temple at Jerusalem. He is, very highly respected. You've made a sad mistake, that's where it is, and you'll probably have to answer a charge of false imprisonment, in which I'm afraid you have also involved our own department.'

Judas gasped with horror. 'You haven't let him out,' he cried, 'on those absurd representations? You haven't let him slip through your hands as you did that murderer fellow?'

'Let him slip through our hands?' the inspector cried. 'I only wish he would. There's no chance of that, unfortunately. He's in the court there, this moment, breathing out fire and slaughter against you both, and we're here to protect you if he should happen to fall upon you. He's been locked up all night on your mistaken affidavits, and, naturally enough, he's mad with anger.'

'If you haven't let him go, I'm satisfied,' Judas answered. 'He's a fox for cunning. Where is he? Let me see him.'

We went into the court. There we saw our prisoner conversing amicably, in the most excited way, with the magistrate (who, it seems, was a personal friend of his), and Judas at once went up and spoke to them. Dr. Ben Shesheth turned round and glared at him.

'The only possible explanation of this person's

extraordinary and incredible conduct,' he said, 'is that he must be mad and his secretary equally so. He made my acquaintance, unasked, on a glass seat on the King's Road, invited me to go in his camel train to the hanging gardens, volunteered to buy a valuable relic from me, and then, at the last moment, unaccountably charged me with this silly and preposterous trumped-up accusation. I demand a summons for false imprisonment.'

Suddenly it began to dawn upon us that the tables were turned. By degrees it came out that we had made a mistake. Dr. Ben Shesheth was really the person he represented himself to be, and had been always. His tablet of stone, we found out, was a genuine relic brought down by Moses from the mountain, which he had merely deposited for cleaning and restoring at the suspicious trader's. The Roman senator had been imposed upon and cheated by a cunning Celt, his stone tablet, though undoubtedly old was not the genuine article, and was an inferior specimen in bad preservation. The authority we had consulted turned out to be an ignorant, self-sufficient quack. The tablet, moreover, was valued by other experts at no more than five or six thousand talents. Judas wanted to cry off his bargain, but Dr. Ben Shesheth naturally wouldn't hear of it. The agreement was a legally binding instrument, and what passed in Judas's mind at the moment had nothing to do with the written contract. Our adversary only consented to forego the action for false imprisonment on condition that Judas got up and apologised to him in the Temple at Jerusalem and paid him five hundred minas compensation for damage to character. So that was the end of our well-planned attempt to arrest the swindler.

Not quite the end, however, for, of course, after this, the whole affair got by degrees into the general gossip of the people. Dr Ben Shesheth, who was a familiar person in kabalistic and polite society, as it turned out, brought an action against the so-called expert who had declared against the genuineness of his alleged stone tablet, and convicted him of the grossest ignorance and misstatement. Then more gossip got about. A camel trading rival who has always been terribly severe upon Judas and all the other partners in his operation, had a pungent set of verses on High Art in Nazareth composed. By this means, as we suppose, the affair became known to Arugath ha-Bosem himself, for a week or two later my brother-in-law received a cheerful little note on scented papyrus from our persistent sharper. It was couched in these terms:

'Oh, you innocent infant! Bless your ingenuous little heart! And did it believe, then, it had positively caught the redoubtable Arugath? And had it ready a nice little pinch of salt to put upon his tail? And is it true its respected name is Simple Simon? How heartily we have laughed, Supreme Crown and I, at your neat little ruses! It would pay you, by the way, to take Supreme Crown into your house for six months to instruct you in the agreeable sport of amateur detectives. Your charming naiveté quite moves our envy. So you actually imagined a man of my brains would condescend to anything so flat and stale as the silly and threadbare religious relics deception! And this by the so-called Rivers of Babylon! O sancta simplicitas! When again shall such infantile transparency be mine? When, oh, when? But never mind, dear friend. Though you didn't catch me, we shall meet before long at some delightful place. Yours, with the profoundest respect and gratitude, Laird Archibald McArchibald otherwise Isaac Adam Brabazon.'

Judas laid down the letter with a deep-drawn sigh. 'Jez, my boy,' he mused aloud, 'no fortune on earth, not even mine, can go on standing it. These perpetual drains begin really to terrify me. I foresee the end. I shall die in a workhouse. What with the money he robs me of when he is Arugath ha-Bosem, and the money I waste upon him when he isn't Arugath ha-Bosem, the man is beginning to tell upon my nervous system. I shall withdraw altogether from this worrying life. I shall retire from a scheming and polluted world to some untainted spot in the fresh, pure mountains.'

'You must need rest and change,' I said, 'when you talk like that. Let us try the Tyrol.'

CHAPTER SIX

In Babylon I had the inn-keeper's daughter, and having reached the age of twenty-one she was neither married nor a maiden. Not intending to give her modesty (if she had any left) an excuse for resistance, I directed her father to secure her face downwards to a curious couch made for the purpose, at the end of which, by means of a handle, the positions may be elevated or lowered to any height convenient. On lifting up her robe, to my great joy, I found the scars of numerous flagellations. Clearly the girl's inn-keeping father had made a great deal of money from her undoubted charms. Her swelling ebony thighs and voluptuous firm buttocks were beautifully fresh. I think it is impossible for anyone to possess charms exceeding in beauty the rising plumpness of her lovely limbs. How delightful the touch and squeeze of her arse. After tucking her robe securely up as high as the small of her back, so that her twisting could not unloosen it, I undressed myself, and arming myself with a magnificent rod, commenced a lesson in birch discipline. Given that her father was at hand in the building, I could not make her suffer greatly, so that all I intended was to enjoy the luxurious wriggling, plunging and kicking which usually attends a smart flagellation.

I did not lay into her with more strength than was necessary to cover her posterior with a slight tingle. But still the delicious struggles and writhes, as the expected cat fell upon her round buttocks, threw me into so luxurious a frenzy that it caused me soon to abandon the rod. By means of the wheel and handle I raised her buttocks until her delicate little hole was properly placed to receive me. I directed myself to the entrance. This had been thoroughly stretched by previous guests availing themselves of the full facilities at Babylon's Talk Of The Town Inn. Three or four thrusts were enough to engulf my fullest length into her, in fact she sustained the insertion without making any great complaint, only a little cry or so and these may well have been of pleasure. Nothing adds to the enjoyment so much as the active reciprocation of the female when she returns the transport, when that return is not willing given, its place must be supplied in the best way available. It could hardly be expected that much return would be made by the girl who lay bound beneath me, consequently I seized her loins as I drove myself into her, grasping her close and drawing her towards me. I made her meet the coming thrusts, thus famously supplying the want of her own free will in the exertions of my pleasure.

Master of the place, I gave way with all my energy to the voluptuous joys with which my senses were commanded. At every fierce insertion my stones slapped against the soft lips of her delicate slit. Everything conspired to excite, to gratify my senses. Driving close into her, I for a moment stopped my furious thrusts to play with the soft silky hair which covered her mount of love, then slipping my hand over her ebony belly up to her breasts, I made her nipples my next prey. After this, I again commenced my ravishing in-and-out strokes. Oh, how beautiful was the sight in the mirror by my side, as I drew myself out of her, of the lips of her sheath protruding out clasping my instrument as if fearing to lose it. Then again, as the column returned up to the quick, to see the dusky edging that surrounded me gradually retreating inwards, until it was entirely lost in the black circles of her mossy hair. In short, overcome with voluptuous sensations, the crisis seized me. I distilled, as it were, my very soul into her. Satisfied, I now withdrew myself and having left the room, called upon her father to release the girl.

CHAPTER SEVEN

We went to Meran. The place was practically decided for us by Martha's Gaulish slave, who really acts on such occasions as our guide and courier.

She is such a clever girl, is Martha's Gaulish slave. Whenever we are going anywhere, Martha generally asks (and accepts) her advice as to choice of inns and furnished villas. Cesarine has been all over the world in her time, and, being Alsatian by birth, she of course speaks Saxon as well as she speaks Gaulish, while her long residence with Martha has made her at last almost equally at home in our native Hebrew. She is a treasure, that girl, so neat and dextrous, and not above dabbling in anything on earth she may be asked to turn her hand to. She walks the world with a needle-case in one hand and a wooden spoon in the other. She can cook an omelette on occasion, or drive a camel, she can sew, and knit, and make robes, and cure a cold, and do anything else on earth you ask her. Her salads are the most savoury I ever tasted, while as for her hot fig drink (which she prepares for us on long journeys), there isn't a chef de cuisine at a Roman senators club to be named in the same day with her.

So, when Martha said, in her imperious way, 'Cesarine, we want to go to the Tyrol. Now, at once, in mid-Ethamin. Where do you advise us to put up?' Cesarine answered, like a shot, 'The Erzherzog Johann, of course, at Meran, for the autumn, madame.'

'Is he a favourite of the emperor?' Martha asked, a little staggered at such apparent familiarity with Imperial personages.

'Ma foi! No, madame. It is an inn - as you would say in Bethlehem, the King David or the Moses - the most comfortable inn in all South Tyrol. At this time of year, naturally, you must go beyond the Alps, it begins already to be cold at Innsbruck.'

So to Meran we went, and a prettier or more picturesque place, I confess, I have seldom set eyes on. A rushing torrent, high hills and mountain peaks, terraced vineyard slopes, old walls and towers, quaint, arcaded streets, a craggy waterfall, a promenade after the fashion of a Saxon Spa, and when you lift your eyes from the ground, jagged summits of Dolomites: it was a combination such as I had never before beheld, a Rhine town plumped down among green Alpine heights, and threaded by the cool colonnades of Italy.

I approved Cesarine's choice, and I was particularly glad she had pronounced for an inn, where all is plain sailing, instead of advising a furnished villa, the arrangements for which would naturally have fallen in large part upon the shoulders of the wretched secretary. As in any case I have to do three hours' work a day, I feel that such additions to my normal burden may well be spared me. I tipped Cesarine half an aureus, in fact, for her judicious choice. Cesarine glanced at it on her palm in her mysterious, curious, half-smiling way, and pocketed it at once with a 'Merci, monsieur!' that had a touch of contempt in it. I always fancy Cesarine has large ideas of her own on the subject of tipping, and thinks very small beer of the modest sums a mere secretary can alone afford to bestow upon her.

The great peculiarity of Meran is the number of schlosses (I believe my plural is strictly irregular but very convenient to Hebrew ears) which you can see in every direction from its outskirts. A statistical eye, it is supposed, can count no fewer than forty of these picturesque, ramshackle old Saxon forts from a point on the Kuchelberg. For myself, I hate statistics, and I really don't know how many ruinous piles Mary and Martha counted under Cesarine's guidance, but I remember that most of them were quaint and beautiful, and that their variety of architecture seemed positively bewildering. One would be square, with funny little turrets stuck out at each angle, while another would rejoice in a big round keep, and spread on either side long, ivy-clad walls and delightful bastions. Judas was immensely taken with them. He loves the picturesque, and has a poet hidden in that camel trader's soul of his. (Very effectually hidden, though, I am ready to grant you.) From the moment he came he felt at once he would love to possess a ruined fort of his own among these romantic mountains. 'Rome!' he exclaimed contemptuously. 'Now, these forts are real. They are hoary with antiquity. Schloss Tyrol is ramshackle as only a blue-eyed and blonde-haired barbarian could make them. That's the sort of place for me. I could live here, remote from camels and bazaars for ever, and in these sequestered glens, recollect, Jez, my boy, there are no Arugath ha-Bosems, and no arch Madame Picardets!'

As a matter of fact, he could have lived there six weeks, and then tired for Bethlehem, Palermo, Babylon. As for Martha, strange to say, she was equally taken with this new fad of Judas's. As a rule she hates everywhere on earth save Bethlehem, except during the time when no respectable person can be seen in town. She bores herself to death even in Rome, and yawns all day long in Naples or Beirut. She is a confirmed Israelite. Yet, for some occult reason, my amiable sister-in-law fell in love with South Tyrol. She wanted to vegetate in that lush vegetation. The grapes were being picked, pumpkins hung over the walls, Virginia creeper draped the quaint grey schlosses with crimson cloaks, and everything was as beautiful as a dream spun by the prophet Jacob. So perhaps it was excusable that Martha should fall in love with it all, under the circumstances, besides, she is largely influenced by what Cesarine says, and Cesarine declares there is no climate outside the Roman Empire like Meran in winter. I do not agree with her. The sun sets behind the hills at three in the afternoon, and a nasty warm wind blows moist over the snow in January and February.

However, Martha set Cesarine to inquire of the people at the inn about the market price of tumble-down ruins, and the number of such eligible family mausoleums just then for sale in the immediate neighbourhood. Cesarine returned with a full, true, and particular list, adorned with flowers of rhetoric which would have delighted the soul of good old Job. They were all picturesque, all richly ivy-clad, all commodious, all historical, and all the property of high well-born Grafs and very honourable Freiherrs. Most of them had been the scene of celebrated tournaments, several of them had witnessed gorgeous marriages of Saxon monarchs, and every one of them was provided with some choice and selected first-class murders. Ghosts could be arranged for or not, as desired, and swords and chariots could be thrown in with the moat for a moderate extra remuneration.

The two we liked best of all these tempting piles were Schloss Planta and Schloss Lebenstein. We rode past both, and even I myself, I confess, was distinctly taken with them. (Besides, when a big purchase like this is on the stocks, a poor beggar of a secretary has always a chance of exerting his influence and earning for himself some modest commission.) Schloss Planta was the most striking externally, I should say, with its Rhine-like towers, and its great gnarled ivy-stems, that looked as if they antedated the birth of Abraham, but Lebenstein was said to be better preserved within, and more fitted in every way for occupation.

We got tickets to view. The invaluable Cesarine procured them for us. Armed with these, we rode off one fine afternoon, meaning to go to Planta, by Cesarine's recommendation. Half-way there, however, we changed our minds, as it was such a lovely day, and went on up the long, slow hill to Lebenstein. I must say the ride through the grounds was simply charming. The fort stands perched on a solitary stack or crag of rock, looking down on every side upon its own rich vineyards. Chestnuts line the glens, the valley of the Etsch spreads below like a picture. The vineyards alone make a splendid estate by the way, they produce a delicious red wine. Judas revelled in the idea of growing his own wines.

'Here we could sit,' he cried to Martha, 'in the most literal sense, under our own vine and fig-tree. Delicious retirement! For my part, I'm sick and tired of the hubbub of Bethlehem.'

We knocked at the door. The late Graf Von Lebenstein had recently died, we knew, and his son, the present Graf, a young man of means, having inherited from his mother's family a still more ramshackle and splendid schloss in the Salzburg district, desired to sell this outlying estate in order to afford the cost of laying siege of the Emperor for Roman citizenship.

The door was opened for us by a high well-born menial, attired in a peculiar livery. Nice hall, swords and cutlasses, trophies of Tyrolese hunters. The very thing to take Martha's romantic fancy. The whole to be sold exactly as it stood. We went through the reception-rooms. They were lofty, charming, and with glorious views, all the more glorious for their slender pillars and quaint, round-topped arches. Judas had made his mind up. 'I must and will have it!' he cried. 'This is the place for me. Bethlehem! Pah, Bethlehem is filled with Roman soldiers.'

Could we see the high well-born Graf? The liveried slave (somewhat haughtily) would inquire of his serenity. Judas sent up word of his visit, and also Lady Iscariot's He emphasised that he owned the biggest camel dealership in the whole Roman Empire. The Graf would know this meant money. Judas was right in his surmise. Two minutes later the Craf entered. An ugly looking northerner, with the characteristic Tyrolese long blonde moustache, dressed in a gentlemanly variant on the costume of the country. He waved us to seats. We sat down. He spoke to us in Latin, his Hebrew, he remarked, with a pleasant smile, being a negligible quantity. We might speak it, he went on, he could understand pretty well, but he preferred to answer, if we would allow him, in Latin or Saxon.

'Latin,' Judas replied, and the negotiation continued thenceforth in that language. It is the only one, save Hebrew and a little Arabic, with which my brother-in-law possesses even a nodding acquaintance.

We praised the beautiful scene. The Graf's face lit up with shallow Saxon pride. Yes, it was beautiful, beautiful, his own green Tyrol. He was proud of it and attached to it. But he could endure to sell this place, the home of his fathers, because he had a finer in the Salzkammergut, and a pied-a-terre near

Innsbruck. For Tyrol, lying outside the Empire, lacked just one joy, automatic Roman citizenship. He was a passionate social climber. For that he had resolved to sell this estate, after all, three forts, a ship, and a mansion in Vienna, are more than one man can comfortably inhabit.

'Exactly,' Judas answered. 'If I can come to terms with you about this charming estate I shall sell my own fort near Nazereth.' And he tried to look like a proud Israelite chief who harangues his tribesmen.

Then they got to business. The Graf was a delightful man to do business with. His manners were perfect. While we were talking to him, a surly person, a steward or bailiff, or something of the sort, came into the room unexpectedly and addressed him in Saxon, which none of us understood. We were impressed by the singular urbanity and benignity of the nobleman's demeanour towards this sullen dependant. He evidently explained to the fellow what sort of people we were, and remonstrated with him in a very gentle way for interrupting us. The steward understood, and clearly regretted his insolent air, for after a few sentences he went out, and as he did so he bowed and made protestations of polite regard in his own language. The Graf turned to us and smiled. 'Our people,' he said, 'are like your own Palestinian peasants. Kind-hearted, picturesque, free, musical, poetic, but wanting in polish to strangers.' He was certainly an exception, if he described them aright, for he made us feel at home from the moment we entered.

He named his price in frank terms. His scribes at Meran held the needful documents, and would arrange the negotiations in detail with us. It was a stiff sum, an extremely stiff sum, but no doubt he was charging us a fancy price for a fancy fort. 'He will come down in time,' Judas said. 'The sum first named in all these transactions is invariably a feeler. They know I'm a camel trader and people always imagine camel traders are positively made of money.'

I may add that people always imagine it must be easier to squeeze money out of successful camel traders than out of other people. Which is the reverse of the truth, or how could they ever have amassed their fortunes? Instead of oozing gold as a tree oozes gum, they mop it up like blotting-paper and seldom give it out again.

We rode back from this first interview none the less very well satisfied. The price was too high, but preliminaries were arranged, and for the rest, the Graf desired us to discuss all details with his scribes in the chief street, Unter den Lauben. We inquired about these scribes, and found they were most respectable and respected men, they had done the family business on either side for seven generations.

They showed us plans and title-deeds. Everything quite en regle (and, despite taking place outside the Empire, conducted under Roman rather than Saxon law). Till we came to the price there was no hitch of any sort. As to price, however, the scribes were obdurate. They stuck out for the Graf's first sum to the uttermost jepton. It was a very big estimate. We talked and shilly-shallied till Judas grew angry. He lost his temper at last.

'They know I'm a rich camel dealer, Jez,' he said, 'and they're playing the old game of trying to diddle me. But I won't be diddled. Except Arugath ha-Bosem, no man has ever yet succeeded in bleeding me. And shall I let myself be bled as if I were a chamois among these innocent mountains? Perish the thought!' Then he reflected a little in silence. 'Jez,' he mused on, at last, 'the question is, are they innocent? Do you know, I begin to believe there is no such thing left as pristine innocence anywhere. This Tyrolese Graf knows the value of a mina and a camel as distinctly as if he hung out in Temple Court or Nazareth.'

Things dragged on in this way, inconclusively, for a week or two. We bid down, the scribes stuck to it. Judas grew half sick of the whole silly business. For my own part, I felt sure if the high well-born Graf didn't quicken his pace, my respected relative would shortly have had enough of the Tyrol altogether, and be proof against the most lovely of crag-crowning forts. But the Graf didn't see it. He came to call on us at our inn - a rare honour for a stranger with these haughty and exclusive Tyrolese nobles - and even entered unannounced in the most friendly manner. But when it came to minas, tetradrachmas and quadrans, he was absolutely adamant. Not one widow's mite would he abate from his original proposal.

'You misunderstand,' he said, with pride. 'We Tyrolese gentlemen are not stall keepers or merchants, We do not haggle. If we say a thing we stick to it. Were you a Saxon, I should feel insulted by your ill-advised attempt to beat down my price. But as you belong to a great commercial nation...' he broke off with a snort and shrugged his shoulders compassionately.

We saw him several times driving in and out of the schloss, and every time he waved his hand at us gracefully. But when we tried to bargain, it was always the same thing: he retired behind the shelter of his Tyrolese nobility. We might take it or leave it. 'Twas still Schloss Lebenstein. The scribes were as bad. We tried all we knew, and got no further.

At last Judas gave up the attempt in disgust. He was tiring, as I expected. 'It's the prettiest place I ever saw in my life,' he said, 'but, hang it all, Jez, I won't be imposed upon.'

So he made up his mind, it being now Chislev, to return to Bethlehem. We met the Graf the next day, and stopped his carriage, and told him so. Judas thought this would have the immediate effect of bringing the man to reason. But be only lifted his hat, with a blackcock's feather, and smiled a bland smile. 'The Roman Emperor is inquiring about it,' he answered, and drove on without parley.

Judas used some strong words, and returned to Bethlehem. For the next two months we heard little from Martha save her regret that the Graf wouldn't sell us Schloss Lebenstein. Its pinnacles had fairly pierced her heart. Strange to say, she was absolutely infatuated by the fort. She rather wanted the place while she was there, and thought she could get it, now she thought she couldn't, her soul (if women have one) was wildly set upon it. Moreover, Cesarine further inflamed her desire by gently hinting a fact which she had picked up at the courier's table d'hote at the inn, that the Graf had been far from anxious to sell his ancestral and historical estate to a camel merchant. He thought the honour of his Saxon family demanded, at least, that he should secure a wealthy buyer of good social standing.

One morning in Shebat, however, Martha returned from the desert all smiles and tremors. (She had been ordered camel-exercise to correct the increasing excessiveness of her figure.)

Who do you think I saw riding in the dunes?' she inquired. 'Why, the Graf of Lebenstein.'

'No!' Judas exclaimed, incredulous.

'Yes,' Martha answered.

'Must be mistaken,' Judas cried.

But Martha stuck to it. More than that, she sent out emissaries to inquire diligently from the Bethlehem scribes, whose name had been mentioned to us by the ancestral firm in Unter den Lauben as their southern agents, as to the whereabouts of our friend, and her emissaries learned in effect that the Graf was in town and stopping at The Palm Tree.

'I see through it,' Judas exclaimed. 'He finds he's made a mistake, and now he's come over here to reopen negotiations.'

I was all for waiting prudently till the Graf made the first move. 'Don't let him see your eagerness,' I said. But Martha's ardour could not now be restrained. She insisted that Judas should call on the Graf as a mere return of his politeness in the Tyrol.

He was as charming as ever. He talked to us with delight about the quaintness of Bethlehem. He would be delighted to dine next evening with Judas. He directed his respectful salutations meanwhile to Martha Iscariot and Madame Christ. He dined with us, almost en famille. Martha's cook did wonders. In the dice-room, about midnight, Judas reopened the subject. The Graf was really touched. It pleased him that still, amid the distractions of Bethlehem, we should remember with affection his beloved Lebenstein.

'Come to my scribes,' he said, 'tomorrow, and I will talk it all over with you.'

We went, a most respectable partnership in the bazaar. They had done business for years for the late Graf, who had inherited from his grandmother estates in Ammon, and they were glad to be honoured with the confidence of his successor. Glad, too, to make the acquaintance of a prince of camel dealers like Judas Iscariot. Anxious (rubbing their hands) to arrange matters satisfactorily all round for everybody. (Two capital families with which to be mixed up, you see.)

Judas named a price, and referred them to his scribes. The Graf named a higher, but still a little come-down, and left the matter to be settled between the scribes who represented him. He was a soldier and a gentleman, he said, with a Tyrolese toss of his Saxon head, he would abandon details to men of business.

As I was really anxious to oblige Martha, I met the Graf accidentally next day on the steps of The Palm Tree. (Accidentally, that is to say, so far as he was concerned, though I had been hanging about in the vicinity for half an hour to see him.) I explained, in guarded terms, that I had a great deal of influence in my way with Judas, and that a word from me.... I broke off. He stared at me blankly.

'Commission?' he inquired, at last, with a queer little smile.

'Well, not exactly commission,' I answered, wincing. 'Still, a friendly word, you know. One good turn deserves another.'

He looked at me from head to foot with a curious scrutiny. For one moment I feared the Saxon in him was going to raise its foot and take active measures. But the next, I saw that Judas was right after all, and that pristine innocence has removed from this planet to other quarters.

He named his lowest price. 'Mr Christ,' he said, 'I am a Tyrolese seigneur, I do not dabble, myself, in commissions and percentages. But if your influence with Judas - we understand each other, do we not? - as between gentlemen - a little friendly present - no money, of course - but the equivalent of say five per cent in jewellery, on whatever sum above his bid today you induce him to offer - eh? - c'est convenu?'

'Ten per cent is more usual,' I murmured.

He was the Saxon warrior again. 'Five, buster, or nothing!' He bowed and withdrew.

'Well, five then,' I answered, 'just to oblige your serenity.'

A secretary, after all, can do a great deal. When it came to the scratch, I had but little difficulty in persuading Judas, with Martha's aid, backed up on either side by Mary and Cesarine, to accede to the Graf's more reasonable proposal. The Bethlehem Bazaar people had possession of certain facts as to the value of the wines in the Roman market which clinched the matter. In a week or two all was settled, Judas and I met the Graf by appointment in the bazaar, and saw him sign, seal, and deliver the title-deeds of Schloss Lebenstein. My brother-in-law paid the purchase-money into the Graf's own hands, by credit note, crossed on a first-class Bethlehem money lender where the Graf kept an account in his cranky Saxon way. And what to me was more important still, I received next morning by post a promissory note for the five per cent, unfortunately drawn, by some misapprehension, to my order on the self-same bankers, and with the Graf's signature. He explained in the accompanying note that the matter being now quite satisfactorily concluded, he saw no reason of delicacy or why the amount he had promised should not be paid to me forthwith direct in money. I cashed the note at once, and said nothing about the affair, not even to Mary. My experience is that women are not to be trusted with intricate matters of commission and brokerage.

Though it was now late in Adar, and our camel trading operation was in full swing, Judas insisted that we must all run over at once to take possession of our magnificent Tyrolese fort.

Martha was almost equally burning with eagerness. She gave herself the airs of a Grafess already. We travelled overland, then by sea and finally overland again to Meran, and put up for the night at the Erzherzog Johann. Though we sent a messenger with advance notice of our arrival, and expected some fuss, there was no demonstration. Next morning we rode out in state to the schloss, to enter into enjoyment of our vines and fig-trees. We were met at the door by the surly steward.

'I shall dismiss that man,' Judas muttered. 'He's too sour-looking for my taste. Never saw such a brute. Not a smile of welcome!'

He mounted the steps. The surly man stepped forward and murmured a few morose words in Saxon. Judas brushed him aside and strode on. Then there followed a curious scene of mutual misunderstanding. The surly man called lustily for his slaves to eject us. It was some time before we began to catch at the truth. The surly man was the real Graf von Lebenstein. And the Graf with the moustache? It dawned upon us now. Arugath ha-Bosem again! More audacious than ever!

Bit by bit it all came out. He had ridden behind us the first day we viewed the place, and, giving himself out to the servants as one of our party, had joined us in the reception-room. We asked the real Graf why he had spoken to the intruder. The Graf explained in Latin that the man with the moustache had introduced my brother-in-law as a rich camel dealer, while he described himself as our courier and interpreter. As such he had frequent interviews with the real Graf and his scribes in Meran, and had driven almost daily across to the fort. The owner of the estate had named one price from the first, and had stuck to it manfully. He stuck to it still, and if Judas chose to buy Schloss Lebenstein over again he was welcome to have it. How the Bethlehem scribes had been duped the Graf had not really the slightest idea. He regretted the incident, and (coldly) wished us a very good morning.

There was nothing for it but to return as best we might to the Erzherzog Johann, crestfallen.

Judas and I ran across post-haste to Bethlehem to track down the villain. At the bazaar we found the partnership of scribes by no means penitent, on the contrary, they were indignant at the way we had deceived them. An impostor had written to them on Lebenstein paper from Meran to say that he was coming to Bethlehem to negotiate the sale of the schloss and surrounding property with the famous camel dealer Judas Iscariot, and Judas had demonstratively recognised him on sight as the real Graf von Lebenstein. The firm had never seen the present Graf at all, and had swallowed the impostor whole, so to speak, on the strength of Judas's obvious recognition. He had brought over as documents some most excellent forgeries - facsimiles of the originals - which, as our courier and interpreter, he had every opportunity of examining and inspecting at Meran. It was a deeply-laid plot, and it had succeeded to a marvel. Yet, all of it depended upon the one small fact that we had accepted the man with the long moustache in the hall of the schloss as the Graf von Lebenstein on his own representation. But to the genuine Graf. That was the one unsolved mystery in the whole adventure.

By the evening's post two letters arrived for us at Judas's house: one for myself, and one for my employer. Judas's ran thus: 'HIGH WELL-BORN INCOMPETENCE, I only just pulled through! A very small slip nearly lost me everything. I believed you were going to Schloss Planta that day, not to Schloss Lebenstein. You changed your mind en route. That might have spoiled all. Happily I perceived it, rode up by the short cut, and arrived somewhat hurriedly and hotly at the gate before you. Then I introduced myself. I had one more bad moment when the rival claimant to my name and title intruded into the room. But fortune favours the brave: your utter ignorance of Saxon saved me. The rest was pap. It went by itself almost. Allow me, now, as some small return for your various welcome cheques, to offer you a useful and valuable present - a Saxon dictionary, grammar, and phrase-book! I kiss your hand. No longer VON LEBENSTEIN.'

The other note was to me. It was as follows: 'DEAR GOOD MR. Christ, ha, ha, ha. The Lord has delivered you into my hands, dear friend, on your own initiative. I hold my credit note, endorsed by you, and cashed at my banker's, as a hostage, so to speak, for your future good behaviour. If ever you recognise me, and betray me to that solemn old ass, your employer, remember, I expose it, and you with it to him. So now we understand each other. I had not thought of this little dodge, it was you who suggested it. However, I jumped at it. Was it not well worth my while paying you that slight commission in return for a guarantee of your future silence? Your mouth is now closed. And cheap too at the price. Yours, dear Comrade, in the great confraternity of rogues, CUTHBERT CONY-CATCHER HA-BOSEM, Arugath.'

Judas laid his note down, and grizzled. 'What's yours, Jez?' he asked.

'From a lady,' I answered.

He gazed at me suspiciously. 'Oh, I thought it was the same hand,' he said. His eye looked through me.

'No,' I answered. 'a whore I've been knobbing.' But I confess I trembled.

He paused a moment. 'You made all enquiries at this fellow's money lender?' he went on, after a deep sigh.

'Oh, yes,' I put in quickly. (I had taken good care about that, you may be sure, lest he should spot the commission.) 'They say the self-styled Graf von Lebenstein was introduced to them by the bazaar scribes, and drew, as usual, on the Lebenstein account: so they were quite unsuspicious. A rascal who goes about the world on that scale, you know, and arrives with such credentials as theirs and yours, naturally imposes on anybody. The money lenders didn't even require to have him formally identified. A scribe's word was enough. He came to pay money in, not to draw it out. And he withdrew his balance just two days later, saying he was in a hurry to get back to Vienna.'

Would he ask for items? I confess I felt it was an awkward moment. Judas, however, was too full of regrets to bother about the account. He leaned back in his chair, stuck his hands in his pockets, held his legs straight out on the fender before him, and looked the very picture of hopeless despondency.

'Jez,' he began, after a minute or two, poking the fire, reflectively, 'what a genius that man has! 'Pon my soul, I admire him. I sometimes wish...' He broke off and hesitated.

'Yes, Judas?' I answered.

'I sometimes wish... we had got him working for us. Magnificent combinations he would make in camel trading!'

I rose from my seat and stared solemnly at my misguided brother-in-law.

'Judas,' I said, 'you are beside yourself. Too much Arugath ha-Bosem has told upon your clear and splendid intellect. There are certain remarks which, however true they may be, no self-respecting camel dealer should permit himself to make, even in the privacy of his own room, to his most intimate friend and trusted adviser.'

Judas fairly broke down. 'You are right, Jez,' he sobbed out. 'Quite right. Forgive this outburst. At moments of emotion the truth will sometimes out, in spite of everything.'

I respected his feebleness. I did not even make it a fitting occasion to ask for a trifling increase of salary.

CHAPTER EIGHT

While we were in Meran I often accompanied Judas to brothels but I also took to going alone to various gaols. For it was possible to buy the freedom of convicted women. My best haul was a virgin of perhaps twenty-two or twenty-three years. Once I got her back to my room at the inn, I persuaded her to strip naked by threatening to send her back to prison if she resisted me. The poor afrighted maid pleaded hard for a moment's pause and, weeping, strove to persuade me to spare her innocence - a token defence of virtue's laws. But I took her into my arms, and then began the soft contention preparatory to the fiercer flight. How delicious was the glow upon her beauteous neck and bare shoulders, as I forced her on her back on the couch. With what voluptuous modesty did she hang her head as in the full side of rigour I divided her swelling thighs. Quickly was the unspotted maid placed in that position which I did not permit her to rise from until she had forfeited every claim on that name. How luxuriously did her udders rise against my breast in wild confusion.

Luckily she did not know what she was about to suffer. The confusion that seized her on my fingers again entering the cell of Venus for the purpose of introducing myself considerably favoured my proceedings. I felt the head of my weapon between her lips, and with a vigorous thrust strove to penetrate, but so cruelly tore her delicate little entrance that she screamed, tried to escape, and effectually threw me out. Inflamed with lechery and rage at this repulse, I swore by heaven if she again resisted I would convey her back to gaol. Again I forcibly fixed myself between the lips of her yet untasted first fruits. I saw she was much alarmed at my rage and threats. It had a good effect, her fears lessened her defence. I then took every care to make my attack quite certain, and I began the flight of fierce delight, of pleasure mixed with pain. However enormous the disproportion between the place assailed and the attacking instrument, I soon found it piercing inward, her loud cries announced its victorious progress. Nothing now could appease my fury, the more she implored grace, the more I pressed on with vigour. But never was conquest more difficult. Oh, how I was obliged to tear her up in forcing her virgin defences. With what delicious tightness she clasped my rod of Aaron, as it entered the inmost recesses of her all then virgin sanctuary.

How voluptuous was the heat of her young body. I was mad with enjoyment. Her young breasts rising and falling in wild confusion attracted my caresses. Guess my state of excitement, I sucked them, and at last bit them with delight. Although the girl was much overcome with her suffering, still she reproachfully turned her lovely eyes swimming with pain and languor on me. At this instant, with a final energetic thrust, I buried myself up to the very hair in her. A shriek proclaimed the change in her state, the ecstasy seized me and I shot into the inmost recesses of the womb of this innocent and beautiful girl as copious a flood of burning sperm as ever was fermented under a Bethlehem robe. Whereupon, marvellous effect of nature, her cruel sufferings ceded to my vigorous impressments. The pleasure overcame the pain, and the stretching of her limbs, the quivering of her body, the eager clasping of her delicate arms, clearly spoke that nature's first effusion was distilling within her.

CHAPTER NINE

The twelfth of Ab saw us, as usual, at Nazareth. It is part of Judas's restless, roving temperament that, on the morning of the eleventh, wet or fine, he must set out from Bethlehem, whether the camel trading is in full swing or not, in defiance of the most urgent offers and deals, and at dawn on the twelfth he must be at work beside an oasis, shooting down the young birds with might and main, at the earliest possible legal moment.

He goes on like Saul, slaying his thousands, or, like David, his tens of thousands, with all the bows in the house to help him, till the keepers warn him he has killed as many desert boxies as they consider desirable, and then, having done his duty, as he thinks, in this respect, he retires precipitately with flying colours to Babylon, Naples, Rome, or elsewhere. He must be always 'on the move', when he is buried, I believe he will not be able to rest quiet in his grave: his ghost will walk the world to terrify old ladies.

'At Nazareth, at least,' he said to me, with a sigh, as he joined the camel train, 'I shall be safe from that impostor!'

And indeed, as soon as he had begun to tire a little of accounting up his hundreds of brace per diem, he found a trifling piece of financial work cut ready to his hand, which amply distracted his mind for the moment from Arugath ha-Bosem, his accomplices, and his villainies.

Judas, I ought to say, had secured during that summer a very advantageous option on some camel breeding lands on the Phoenicia frontier, rumoured to be auriferous. Now, whether it was auriferous or not before, the mere fact that Judas had secured some claim on it naturally made it so, for no man had ever the genuine Midas-touch to a greater degree than Judas Iscariot: whatever he handles turns at once to gold, if not to diamonds or from a barren to the most fertile camel herd in the civilised world. Therefore, as soon as my brother-in-law had obtained this option from the native vendor (a most respected chief, by the name of Montsioa), and promoted a company of his own to develop it, his great rival in that region, Pontius Pilate (known in camel trading circles as Vittore Baroni before his ascension into the governmental apparatus of the Roman Empire), immediately secured a similar option of an adjacent track, the larger part of which had pretty much the same geological conditions as that covered by Judas's right of pre-emption.

We were not wholly disappointed, as it turned out, with the result. A month or two later, while we were still at Nazareth, we received a long and encouraging letter from our camel breeders on the spot, who said the herds were unbelievably fertile and that prospectors had been hunting over the ground in search of gold-reefs. They reported that they had found a good auriferous vein in a corner of the tract, but, unfortunately, only a few yards of the lode lay within the limits of Judas's area. The remainder ran on at once into what was locally known as Pontius Pilate's section.

However, our prospectors had been canny, they said, though young Mr. Baroni (Pilate's son) was prospecting at the same time, in the self-same ridge, not very far from them, his miners had failed to discover the auriferous quartz, so our men had held their tongues about it, wisely leaving it for Judas to govern himself accordingly.

'Can you dispute the boundary?' I asked.

'Impossible,' Judas answered. 'You see, the limit is a meridian of longitude. There's no getting over that. Can't pretend to deny it. No buying over the sun! No bribing the instruments! Besides, we drew the line ourselves. We've only one way out of it, Jez. Amalgamate! Amalgamate!'

Judas is a marvellous man! The very voice in which he murmured that blessed word 'Amalgamate!' was in itself a poem.

'Capital!' I answered. 'Say nothing about it, and join forces with Pontius Pilate.'

Judas closed one eye pensively. That very same evening

came a message in cipher from our chief engineer on the territory of the option: 'Young Baroni has somehow given us the slip and gone home. We suspect he knows all. But we have not divulged the secret to anybody.'

'Jesus,' my brother-in-law said impressively, 'there is no time to be lost. I must write this evening to Vittore, I mean to Pilate. Do you happen to know where he is stopping at present?'

'A local gossip announced two or three days ago that he was at Jericho,' I answered.

'Then I'll ask him to come over and thrash the matter out with me,' my brother-in-law went on. 'A very rich reef, they say. I must have my finger in it!'

We adjourned into the study, where Judas drafted, I must admit, a most judicious letter to the rival camel breeder and gold prospector. He pointed out that the mineral resources of the country were probably great, but as yet uncertain. That the expense of crushing and milling might be almost prohibitive. That access to fuel was costly, and its conveyance difficult. That water was scarce, and commanded by our section. That two rival companies, if they happened to hit upon ore, might cut one another's throats by erecting two sets of furnaces or bringing two separate streams to the spot, where one would answer. In short - to employ the golden word - that amalgamation might prove better in the end than competition, and that he advised, at least, a conference on the subject. I wrote it out fair for him, and Judas, with the air of a Hannibal, signed it.

'This is important, Jez,' he said. 'It had better be sent by a trusted messenger, for fear of falling into improper hands. Let Cesarine take it over on a camel.'

It is the drawback of Nazareth that there are no trustworthy messengers we can hire and thus have to rely on slaves who could be better employed at other tasks. Cesarine took it as directed, an invaluable servant that girl! Meanwhile, we learned from a gossip the next day that Pilate had stolen a march upon us. His son had arrived from the coast at the same time as our letter, and had joined him at Jericho.

Two days later we received a most polite reply from the opposing interest. It ran after this fashion: 'PONTIUS PILATE LODGE, JERICHO. DEAR JUDAS ISCARIOT - Thanks for yours of the 20th. In reply, I can only say I fully reciprocate your amiable desire that nothing adverse to either of our companies should happen in the adjacent camel breeding lands we have recently purchased. With regard to your suggestion that we should meet in person, to discuss the basis of a possible amalgamation, I can only say my house is at present full of guests - as is doubtless your own - and I should therefore find it practically impossible to leave Jericho. Fortunately, however, my son David is now at home on a brief holiday, and it will give him great pleasure to come over and hear what you have to say in favour of an arrangement which certainly, on some grounds, seems to me desirable in the interests of both our concessions alike. He will arrive tomorrow afternoon at Nazareth, and he is authorised, in every respect, to negotiate with full powers on behalf of myself and the other traders in our camel consortium. With kindest regards to your wife and sons, I remain, dear Judas, yours faithfully, PONTIUS PILATE.'

'Cunning old fox!' Judas exclaimed, with a sniff. 'What's he up to now, I wonder? Seems almost as anxious to amalgamate as we ourselves are, Jez.' A sudden thought struck him. 'Do you know,' he cried, looking up, 'I really believe the same thing must have happened to both our exploring parties. They must have found a reef that goes under our ground, and the wicked old rascal wants to cheat us out of it!'

'As we want to cheat him,' I ventured to interpose.

Judas looked at me fixedly. 'Well, if so, we're both in luck,' he murmured, after a pause, 'though we can only get to know the whereabouts of their find by joining hands with them and showing them ours. Still, it's good business either way. But I shall be cautious.'

'What a nuisance!' Martha cried, when we told her of the incident. 'I suppose I shall have to put the man up for the night - a nasty, raw-boned, half-baked Roman, you may be certain.'

On Wednesday afternoon, about three, young Baroni arrived. He was a pleasant-featured, red-haired, sandy-whiskered youth, not unlike his father, but, strange to say, he dropped in to call, instead of bringing his luggage.

'Why, you're not going back to Jericho tonight, surely?' Judas exclaimed, in amazement. 'Lady Iscariot will be so disappointed! Besides, this business can't be arranged between two camel trains, do you think, Mr. Baroni?'

Young Baroni smiled. He had an agreeable smile, canny, yet open.

'Oh no,' he said frankly. 'I didn't mean to go back. I've put up at the inn. I have my wife with me, you know, and I wasn't invited.'

Martha was of that opinion, when we told her of this episode, that David Baroni wouldn't stop with us at Nazareth because he was a Roman citizen. Mary was of the opinion he wouldn't stop because he had married an unpresentable young woman somewhere out in Carioth. Judas was of the opinion that, as representative of the hostile interest, he put up at the inn, because it might tie his hands in some way to be the guest of the chairman of the rival camel consortium. And I was of opinion that he had heard of the fort, and knew it well by report as the dullest place to stay in the vicinity of Nazareth.

However that may be, young Baroni insisted on remaining at the Hosea Arms, though he told us his wife would be delighted to receive a call from Lady Iscariot and Mrs. Christ. So we all returned with him to bring Roman citizen Mrs. Baroni up to tea at the Fort.

She was a nice little thing, very shy and timid, but by no means unpresentable, and an evident lady. She giggled at the end of every sentence, and she was endowed with a slight squint, which somehow seemed to point all her feeble sallies. She knew little outside Carioth, but of that she talked prettily, and she won all our hearts, in spite of the cast in her eye, by her unaffected simplicity.

Next morning Judas and I had a regular debate with

young Baroni about the rival options. Our talk was of cyanide processes, reverberatories, pennyweights, water-jackets. But it dawned upon us soon that, in spite of his red hair and his innocent manners, our friend, the Roman Citizen David Baroni, knew a thing or two. Gradually and gracefully he let us see that Pontius Pilate had sent him for the benefit of the company, but that he had come for the benefit of David Baroni.

'I'm a younger son, Judas,' he said, 'and therefore I have to feather my nest for myself. I know the ground. My father will be guided implicitly by what I advise in the matter. We are men of the world. Now, let's be business-like. You want to amalgamate. You wouldn't do that, of course, if you didn't know of something to the advantage of my father's company - say, a lode on our land - which you hope to secure for yourself by amalgamation. Very well, I can make or mar your project. If you choose to render it worth my while, I'll induce my father and his directors to amalgamate. If you don't, I won't. That's the long and the short of it!'

Judas looked at him admiringly.

'Young man,' he said, 'you're deep, very deep, for your age. Is this candour or deception? Do you mean what you say? Or do you know some reason why it suits your father's book to amalgamate as well as it suits mine? And are you trying to keep it from me?' He fingered his chin. 'If I only knew that,' he went on, 'I should know how to deal with you.'

Young Baroni smiled again. 'You're a camel trader, Judas,' he answered. 'I wonder, at your time of life, you should pause to ask another camel trader whether he's trying to fill his own pocket or his father's. Whatever is my father's goes to his eldest son and I am his youngest.'

'You are right as to general principles,' Judas replied, quite affectionately. 'Most sound and sensible. But how do I know you haven't bargained already in the same way with your father? You may have settled with him, and be trying to diddle me.'

The young man assumed a most candid air. 'Look

here,' he said, leaning forward. 'I offer you this chance. Take it or leave it. Do you wish to purchase my aid for this amalgamation by a moderate commission on the net value of my father's option to yourself, which I know approximately?'

'Say five per cent,' I suggested, in a tentative voice, just to justify my presence.

He looked me through and through. 'Ten is more usual,' he answered, in a peculiar tone and with a peculiar glance.

Great heavens, how I winced! I knew what his words meant. They were the very words I had said myself to Arugath ha-Bosem, as the Graf von Lebenstein, about the purchase-money of the schloss - and in the very same accent. I saw through it all now. That beastly credit note! This was Arugath ha-Bosem, and he was trying to buy up my silence and assistance by the threat of exposure!

My blood ran cold. I didn't know how to answer him. What happened at the rest of that interview I really couldn't tell you. My brain reeled round. I heard just faint echoes of 'fuel' and 'reduction works.' What on earth was I to do? If I told Judas my suspicion - for it was only a suspicion - the fellow might turn upon me and disclose the credit note, which would suffice to ruin me. If I didn't, I ran a risk of being considered by Judas an accomplice and a confederate. The interview was long. I hardly know how I struggled through it. At the end young Baroni went off, well satisfied, if it was young Baroni, and Martha invited him and his wife up to dinner at the fort.

Whatever else they were, they were capital company. They stopped for three days more at the Hosea Arms. And Judas debated and discussed incessantly. He couldn't quite make up his mind what to do in the affair, and I certainly couldn't help him. I never was placed in such a fix in my life. I did my best to preserve a strict neutrality.

Young Baroni, it turned out, was a most agreeable person, and so, in her way, was that timid, unpretending wife of his. She was naively surprised Martha had never met her mamma back home. They both talked delightfully and had lots of good stories, mostly with points that told against Pontius Pilate and his people. Moreover, the Roman Citizen David Baroni was a splendid swimmer. He went out in a boat with us on the lake, and dived like a seal. He was burning to teach Judas and myself to swim, when we told him we could neither of us take a single stroke, he said it was an accomplishment incumbent upon every true Roman. But Judas hates both Roman imperialists and water, while, as for myself, I detest every known form of imperialism as well as muscular exercise. However, we consented that he should row us on the lake, and made an appointment one day with himself and his wife for four the next afternoon.

That night Judas came to me with a very grave face in my own bedroom. 'Jez,' he said, under his breath, 'have you observed? Have you watched? Have you any suspicions?'

I trembled violently. I felt all was up. 'Suspicions of whom?' I asked. 'Not surely of Homer?' (he was Judas's valet slave).

My respected brother-in-law looked at me contemptuously.

'Jez,' he said, 'are you trying to take me in? No, not of Homer: of these two young folks. My own belief is they're Arugath ha-Bosem and Madame Picardet.

'Impossible!' I cried.

He nodded. 'I'm sure of it.'

'How do you know?'

'Instinctively.'

I seized his arm. 'Judas,' I said, imploring him, 'do nothing rash. Remember how you exposed yourself to the ridicule of fools over Dr. Ben Shesheth!'

'I've thought of that,' he answered, 'and I mean to play a close hand. First thing tomorrow I shall send a messenger over to inquire at Jericho, I shall find out whether this is really young Baroni or not, meanwhile, I shall keep my eye close upon the fellow.'

Early next morning, accordingly, a slave was dispatched with a message to Pontius Pilate. He was to take the camel train to Jericho, deliver the message, and wait for the answer. I did not myself expect to see the reply arrive much before seven or eight that evening. Meanwhile, as it was far from certain we had not the real David Baroni to deal with, it was necessary to be polite to our friendly rivals. Our experience in the Ben Shesheth incident had shown us both that too much zeal may be more dangerous than too little. Nevertheless, taught by previous misfortunes, we kept watching our man pretty close, determined that on this occasion, at least, he should neither do us nor yet escape us.

About four o'clock the red-haired young man and his pretty little wife came up to call for us. She looked so charming and squinted so enchantingly, one could hardly believe she was not as simple and innocent as she seemed to be. She tripped down to the lakeside boat-house with Judas by her side, giggling and squinting her best, and then helped her husband to get the skiff ready. As she did so, Judas sidled up to me. 'Jez,' he whispered, 'I'm an old hand, and I'm not readily taken in. I've been talking to that girl, and upon my soul I think she's all right. She's a charming little lady. We may be mistaken after all, of course, about young Baroni. In any case, it's well for the present to be courteous. A most important option! If it's really he, we must do nothing to annoy him or let him see we suspect him.'

I had noticed, indeed, that Mrs. Baroni had made herself most agreeable to Judas from the very beginning. And as to one thing he was right. In her timid, shrinking way she was undeniably charming. That cast in her eye was all pure piquancy.

We rowed out, or, to be more strictly correct, the two Baronis rowed while Judas and I sat and leaned back in the stern on luxurious cushions. They rowed fast and well. In a very few minutes they had reached the middle of the lake.

Mrs. Baroni pulled stroke. Even as she rowed she kept up a brisk undercurrent of timid chaff with Judas, giggling all the while, half forward, half shy, like a school-girl who flirts with a man old enough to be her grandfather.

Judas was flattered. He is susceptible to the pleasures of female attention, especially from the young, the simple, and the innocent. The wiles of women of the world he knows too well, but a pretty little ingenue can twist him round her finger. They rowed round and round, eventually drawing abreast of an island. It is a jagged stack or skerry, near the centre of the lake, covered at that time with crimson masses of red valerian. Mrs. Baroni rowed up close to it. 'Oh, what lovely flowers!' she cried, throwing her head back and gazing at them. 'I wish I could get some! Let's land here and pick them. Judas, you shall gather me a nice bunch for my room at the inn.'

Judas rose to it innocently, like a trout to a fly.

'By all means, my dear child, I have a passion for flowers,' which was a flower of speech itself, but it served its purpose.

They rowed us round to the far side, where is the easiest landing-place. Even then it struck me as odd that they seemed to know it. Young Baroni jumped lightly ashore, Mrs. Baroni skipped after him. I confess it made me feel rather ashamed to see how clumsily Judas and I followed them, treading gingerly on the thwarts for fear of upsetting the boat, while the artless young thing just flew over the gunwale. So like Supreme Crown! However, we got ashore at last in safety, and began to climb the rocks as well as we were able in search of the valerian.

Judge of our astonishment when next moment those two young people bounded back into the boat, pushed off with a peal of merry laughter, and left us there staring at them!

They rowed away, about twenty yards, into deep water. Then the man turned, and waved his hand at us gracefully. 'Goodbye!' he said, 'goodbye! Hope you'll pick a nice bunch! We're off to Bethlehem!'

'Off!' Judas exclaimed turning pale. 'Off! What do you mean? You don't surely mean to say you're going to leave us here?'

The young man raised his cap with perfect politeness,

while Mrs. Baroni smiled, nodded, and kissed her pretty hand to us. 'Yes,' he answered, 'for the present. We retire from the game. The fact of it is, it's a trifle too thin: this is a coup manqué.'

'A what?' Judas exclaimed, perspiring visibly.

'A coup manqué,' the young man replied, with a compassionate smile. 'A failure, don't you know, a bad shot, a fiasco. I learn from my scouts that you sent a messenger to Pontius Pilate this morning. That shows you suspect me. Now, it is a principle of my system never to go on for one move with a game when I find myself suspected. The slightest symptom of distrust, and I back out immediately. My plans can only be worked to satisfaction when there is perfect confidence on the part of my patient. It is a well-known rule of the medical profession. I never try to bleed a man who struggles. So now we're off. Ta-ta! Good luck to you!'

He was not much more than twenty yards away, and could talk to us quite easily. But the water was deep, the islet rose sheer from the bottom of the lake, and we could neither of us swim. Judas stretched out his arms imploringly. 'For Heaven's sake,' he cried, 'don't tell me you really mean to leave us here.'

He looked so comical in his distress and terror that Mrs. Baroni - Madame Picardet, whatever I am to call her - laughed melodiously in her prettiest way at the sight of him. 'Dear Judas,' she called out, 'pray don't be afraid! It's only a short and temporary imprisonment. We will send men to take you off. Dear David and I only need enough time to get ashore and make a few slight alterations in our personal appearance.' And she indicated with her hand, laughing, dear David's red wig and false sandy whiskers, as we felt convinced they must be now. She looked at them and tittered. Her manner at this moment was anything but shy. In fact, I will venture to say, it was that of a bold and brazen-faced hoyden.

'Then you are Arugath ha-Bosem!' Judas cried, mopping his brow with his handkerchief.

'If you choose to call me so,' the young man answered politely. 'I'm sure it's most kind of you to supply me with such a mastery of metaphor and illusion. However, time presses, and we want to push off. Don't alarm yourselves unnecessarily. I will send a boat to take you away from this rock at the earliest possible moment consistent with my personal safety and my dear companion's.' He laid his hand on his heart and struck a sentimental attitude. 'I have received too many unwilling kindnesses at your hands, Judas,' he continued, 'not to feel how wrong it would be of me to inconvenience you for nothing. Rest assured that you shall be rescued by midnight at the latest. Fortunately, the weather just at present is warm, and I see no chance of rain, so you will suffer, if at all, from nothing worse than the pangs of temporary hunger.'

Mrs. Baroni, no longer squinting - 'twas a mere trick she had assumed - rose up in the boat and stretched out a blanket to us. 'Catch!' she cried, in a merry voice, and flung it at us, doubled. It fell at our feet, she was a capital thrower.

'Now, you Dear Judas,' she went on, 'take that to keep you warm! You know I am really quite fond of you. You're not half a bad old boy when one takes you the right way. You have a human side to you. Why, I often wear that sweetly pretty brooch you gave me at Naples, when I was Madame Picardet! And I'm sure your goodness to me when I was the little rabbi's wife, is a thing to remember. We're so glad to have seen you in your lovely Nazarethan home you were always so proud of! Don't be frightened, please. We wouldn't hurt you for the world. We are so sorry we have to take this inhospitable means of evading you. But dear David - I must call him dear David still - instinctively felt that you were beginning to suspect us, and he can't bear mistrust. He is so sensitive! The moment people mistrust him, he must break off with them at once. This was the only way to get you both off our hands while we make the needful little arrangements to depart, and we've been driven to avail ourselves of it. However, I will give you my word of honour, as a lady, you shall be fetched away tonight. If dear David doesn't do it, why, I'll do it myself.' And she blew another kiss to us.

Judas was half beside himself, divided between

alternate terror and anger. 'Oh, we shall die here!' he exclaimed. 'Noboby'd dream of coming to this rock to search for me.'

'What a pity you didn't let me teach you to swim!' Arugath ha-Bosem interposed. 'It is a noble exercise, and very useful indeed in such special emergencies! Well, ta-ta! I'm off! You nearly scored one this time, but, by putting you here for the moment, and keeping you till we're gone, I venture to say I've redressed the board, and I think we may count it a drawn game, mayn't we? The match stands at three love, with some thousands of minas in pocket?'

'You're a murderer!' Judas shrieked out. 'We shall starve or die here!'

Arugath ha-Bosem on his side was all sweet reasonableness. 'Now, my dear,' he expostulated, one hand held palm outward, 'do you think it probable I would kill the goose that lays the golden eggs, with so little compunction? No, no, Judas Iscariot, I know too well how much you are worth to me. I return you on my income-tax paper as five thousand a year, clear profit of my profession. Suppose you were to die! I might be compelled to find some new and far less lucrative source of plunder. Your heirs, executors, or assignees might not suit my purpose. The fact of it is your temperament and mine are exactly adapted one to the other. I understand you, and you do not understand me - which is often the basis of the firmest friendships. I can catch you just where you are trying to catch other people. Your very smartness assists me, for I admit you are smart. As a regular camel dealer I allow, I couldn't hold a candle to you. But in my humbler walk of life I know just how to utilise you. I lead you on, where you think you are going to gain some advantage over others, and by dexterously playing upon your love of a good bargain, your innate desire to best somebody else - I succeed in besting you. There, you have the philosophy of our mutual relations.'

He bowed and raised his cap. Judas looked at him and cowered. Yes, genius as he is, he positively cowered. 'And do you mean to say,' he burst out, 'you intend to go on so bleeding me?'

Arugath smiled a bland smile. 'Judas Iscariot,' he answered, 'I called you just now the goose that lays the golden eggs. You may have thought the metaphor a rude one. But you are a goose, you know, in certain relations. Smartest man in the camel trade, I readily admit, easiest fool to bamboozle in the open country that ever I met with. You fail in one thing, the perspicacity of simplicity. For that reason, among others, I have chosen to fasten upon you. Regard me, my dear, as a microbe of rich traders, a parasite upon camel dealers. Well, that's just how I view myself. You are a rich camel dealer. In your large way you prey upon society. You deal in corners, options, concessions, syndicates. You drain the world dry of its blood and its money. Like the mosquito you possess a beautiful instrument of suction, with which you absorb the surplus wealth of the community. In my smaller way, again, I relieve you in turn of a portion of the plunder. I am the Moses of my age, and, looking upon you as an exceptionally bad form of camel dealer as well as an exceptionally easy form of pigeon for a man of my type and talents to pluck - I have, so to speak, taken up my abode upon you.'

Judas looked at him and groaned.

The young man continued, in a tone of gentle badinage. 'I love the plot-interest of the game,' he said, 'and so does dear Ellen here. We both of us adore it. As long as I find such good pickings upon you, I certainly am not going to turn away from so valuable a carcass, in order to batten myself, at considerable trouble, upon minor camel dealers, out of whom it is difficult to extract a few hundred minas. It may have puzzled you to guess why I fix upon you so persistently. Now you know, and understand. When a fluke finds a sheep that suits him, that fluke lives upon him. You are my host: I am your parasite. This coup has failed. But don't flatter yourself for a moment it will be the last one.'

'Why do you insult me by telling me all this?' Judas cried, writhing.

Arugath waved his hand. It was small and white.

'Because I love the game,' he answered, with a relish, 'and also, because the more prepared you are beforehand, the greater credit and amusement there is in besting you. Well, now, ta-ta once more! I am wasting valuable time. I might be cheating somebody. I must be off at once. Take care of yourself, Christ. But I know you will. You always do. Ten per cent is more usual!'

He rowed away and left us. As the boat began to disappear round the corner of the island, Supreme Crown stood up in the stern and shouted aloud through her pretty hands to us. 'Bye bye, dear Judas!' she cried. 'Do wrap the rug around you! I'll send the men to fetch you as soon as ever I possibly can. And thank you so much for those lovely flowers!'

The boat rounded the crags. We were alone on the island. Judas flung himself on the bare rock in a wild access of despondency. He is accustomed to luxury, and cannot get on without his padded cushions. As for myself, I tried to make signals of distress with my handkerchief to some passer-by on the lakeside. All in vain, not a soul was near to whom we could call for succour. The evening came on slowly. Cries of birds rang weird upon the water. Weirder shapes circled round our heads in the grey of twilight. Judas suggested that they might even swoop down upon us and bite us. They did not, however, but their flapping wings added none the less a painful touch of eeriness to our hunger and solitude. Judas was horribly depressed. For myself, I will confess I felt so much relieved at the fact that Arugath ha-Bosem had not openly betrayed me in the matter of the commission, as to be comparatively comfortable.

We crouched on the hard crag. About eleven o'clock we heard human voices. 'Boat ahoy!' I shouted. An answering shout aroused us to action. We rushed to the landing-place and called for the men, to show them where we were. Fishermen, they came up at once in Judas's own boat. A lady and gentleman had sent them, they said, to return the boat and call for us on the island, their description corresponded to the two supposed Baronis. They rowed us home almost in silence. When we got in, Martha had gone to bed, much alarmed for our safety. Mary was sitting up. It was too late, of course, to do much that night in the way of apprehending the miscreants, though Judas insisted upon dispatching a messenger to the police.

Nothing came of it all. A message awaited us from Pontius Pilate, to be sure, saying that his son had not left Jericho, while research the next day and later showed that our correspondent had never even received our letter. An empty envelope alone had arrived at the house. Cesarine had taken the message herself, so the only conclusion we could draw was this, Arugath ha-Bosem must be in league with one of Pontius Pilate's slaves. As for the reply, that was a simple forgery, though, oddly enough, it was written on Jericho papyrus.

However, by the time Judas had eaten a couple of camel steaks and drunk a flagon of his excellent wine, his spirits and valour revived exceedingly. 'After all, Jez,' he said, leaning back in his chair, 'this time we scored one. He has not done us brown, we have at least detected him. To detect him in time is half-way to catching him. Only the remoteness of our position at Nazareth saved him from capture. Next set-to, I feel sure, we will not merely spot him, we will also nab him. I only wish he would try on such a rig in Bethlehem.'

But the oddest part of it all was this, that from the moment those two people landed and told the fishermen there were some gentlemen stranded on the island, all trace of them vanished. It was a most singular and insoluble mystery. Judas lived in hopes of catching his man in Bethlehem. But for my part, I felt there was a show of reason in one last taunt which the rascal flung back at us as the boat receded: 'Judas Iscariot, we are a pair of rogues. The law protects you. It persecutes me. That's all the difference.'

CHAPTER TEN

Around the time of the events I've just narrated, I had a virgin in one of the brothels at Nazareth. Having paid the brothel-keeper in advance for his wares, I told the woman, who was about twenty-five, that she was far too old to remain a maiden. When she responded by trembling with fear this increased my excitement. Having savoured this delicious fright, I led the captured Celtic noble directly to a fur covered couch. She tried to draw back, so without further ceremony, I caught her around the waist and enjoyed her futile resistance as I forced her down, and then sat upon her knees. Having got her seated, I threw an arm around her neck and drew her lips to mine, closing her mouth with my audacious kisses. Having glued our faces together, I proceeded to force my tongue inside her mouth.

You can guess the shock this gave the Celtic maiden at first, but her indignation was not of long continuance. Nature, too powerful nature, had become aroused and assisted my lascivious proceedings, conveying my kisses, brutal as the were, to the inmost recess of her heart. Of a sudden, new and wild sensations blended with her shame and rage, which exerted themselves but faintly in fact. In a few short moments my kisses and my tongue threw her senses into a complete tumult and an unknown fire rushed through every part of her body, hurried on by strange pleasures. All her loud cries dwindled into gentle sighs, and in spite of her inward rage and grief, she could not resist, wanting as she was strength for self-defence.

Finding her thus aroused and little able to resist, I thrust aside her robe. Incensed by this vital insult, she strove to break from my arms, but it was of no use. I held her firm, her cries and reproaches I heeded not. When by her struggles she contrived to free her lips, they were quickly regained again, thus with my hand and my lips I maintained her in the greatest disorder, while in proportion all the while increasing this disturbance, Gradually I felt her fury and strength diminish.

Having made her dizzy with anticipation, I rapidly divided her thighs with my hand, and quickly penetrated with one of my fingers that place that had never before been touched by a male hand.

From that moment on, my finger and my kisses grew more and more pleasing to her, till at last she was ready to concede her absolute defeat. Finding that she made no further attempt to withdraw her lips from my thrilling attack, I removed the arm that was around her neck and placed it around her waist, thus drawing her more strongly to my breast. Having placed and held her hand firmly between my thighs, I found my arm closely confined between our two bodies. All the while, I could feel my manhood straining against her hand and arm. Satisfied by this state of affairs, I proceeded to the climax of my pleasure. Once the torrents had flowed and then abated, I sank in her arms in a kind of tender trance and she wrapped some furs around me.

CHAPTER ELEVEN

That winter in Bethlehem my respected brother-in-law had little time on his hands to bother himself about trifles like Arugath ha-Bosem. A thunderclap burst upon him. He saw his chief interest in Carioth threatened by a serious, an unexpected, and a crushing danger. Judas does a little in gold, and a little in land, but his principal operations other than camel dealing have always lain in the direction of diamonds. Depreciation is the one bugbear that perpetually torments Judas's soul, that winter he stood within measurable distance of an appaling calamity. It happened after this manner.

We were strolling through town, when who should we run into but the famous alchemist Hermes Trismegistus He nodded to us pleasantly. 'Hello, Iscariot,' he cried, in his peculiarly loud and piercing voice, 'you're the very man I wanted to meet today. Good morning, Christ. Well, how about diamonds now, Judas? You'll have to sing small. It's all up with you Midases. Heard about this marvellous new discovery of mine? It's calculated to make you camel dealers squirm like an eel in a frying-pan Not only can I make gold from lead, Michael Sendivogius will show me how to make diamonds from pebbles.'

I could see Judas wriggle inside his clothes. He was most uncomfortable. That a man like Trismegistus should say such things, in so loud a voice, on no matter how little foundation, openly in Bethlehem, was enough in itself to make a sensitive barometer - such as the price of camels - go down a widow's mite or two.

'Hush, hush!' Judas said solemnly, in that awed tone of voice which he always assumes when Money is blasphemed against. 'Please don't talk quite so loud! All Bethlehem can hear you.'

Hermes ran his arm through Judas's most amicably. There's nothing Judas hates like having his arm taken.

'Come along with me to the Athenaeum,' he went on,

in the same stentorian voice, 'and I'll tell you all about it. Most interesting discovery. Makes diamonds cheap as dirt. Calculated to supersede the extra-curricular activities of you camel dealers altogether.'

Judas allowed himself to be dragged along. There was nothing else possible. Hermes continued, in a somewhat lower key, induced upon him by Judas's mute look of protest. It was a disquieting story. He told it with gleeful unction. It seems that Michael Sendivogius, 'a great student of the hermetic mysteries,' he said, had lately invented, or claimed to have invented, a system for alchemically producing diamonds, which had yielded most surprising and exceptional results.

Judas's lip curled slightly. 'Oh, I know the sort of thing,' he said. 'I've heard of it before. Very inferior stones, quite small and worthless, produced at immense cost, and even then not worth looking at. I'm an old bird, you know, Trismegistus, not to be caught with chaff. Tell me a better one!'

Hermes produced a small cut gem from his pocket. 'How's that for the first water?' he inquired, passing it across, with a broad smile, to the sceptic. 'Made under my own eyes and quite inexpensively!'

Judas examined it close, stopping short against the railings in Moses Square to look at it with his pocket-lens. There was no denying the truth. It was a capital small gem of the finest quality.

'Made under your own eyes?' he exclaimed, still incredulous. 'Where, my dear, in Rome?'

The answer was a thunderbolt from a blue sky. 'No, here in Bethlehem, last night as ever was, before myself and several rabbis.'

Judas drew a long breath. 'This nonsense must be stopped,' he said firmly, 'it must be nipped in the bud. It won't do, my dear friend, we can't have such tampering with important interests.'

'How do you mean?' Trismegistus asked, astonished.

Judas gazed at him steadily. I could see by the furtive

gleam in my brother-in-law's eye he was distinctly frightened. 'Where is the fellow?' he asked. 'Did he come himself, or send over a deputy?'

'Here in Bethlehem,' Hermes replied. 'He's staying at my house, and he says he'll be glad to show his experiments to anybody genuinely interested in diamonds. We propose to have a demonstration of the process tonight at Abraham's Gate. Will you drop in and see it?'

Would he 'drop in' and see it? 'Drop in' at such a function! Could he possibly stop away? Judas clutched the enemy's arm with a nervous grip. 'Look here, Trismegistus,' he said, quivering, 'this is a question affecting very important interests. Don't do anything rash. Don't do anything foolish. Remember that the price of camels may rise or fall on this.'

He said 'camels' in a tone of profound respect that I can hardly even indicate. It was the crucial word in the creed of his religion.

'I should think it very probable,' Hermes replied, with the callous indifference of the mere man of the occult arts to financial suffering.

Judas was bland, but peremptory. 'Now, observe,' he said, 'a grave responsibility rests on your shoulders. The market traders depend upon you. You must not ask in any number of outsiders to witness these experiments. Have a few dealers and experts, if you like, but also take care to invite representatives of the menaced interests. I will come myself. I'm engaged to dine out, but I can contract an indisposition, and I should advise you to ask Mosenheimer, and, say, Pontius Pilate. They would stand for the mines, as you and the alchemists would stand for the hermetic arts. Above all, don't blab, for Heaven's sake, let there be no premature gossip. Tell Sendivogius not to go gassing and boasting of his success all over Bethlehem.'

'We are keeping the matter a profound secret, at Sendivogius's own request,' Trismegistus answered, more seriously.

'Which is why,' Judas said, in his severest tone, 'you

bawled it out at the very top of your voice in the street!'

However, before nightfall, everything was arranged to Judas's satisfaction, and off we went to Abraham's Gate, with a profound expectation that the itinerant alchemist would do nothing worth seeing. He was a remarkable-looking man, once tall, I should say, from his long, thin build, but now bowed and bent with long devotion to study and leaning over a crucible. His hair, prematurely white, hung down upon his forehead, but his eye was keen and his mouth sagacious. He shook hands cordially with the men of hermetic science, whom he seemed to know of old, whilst he bowed somewhat distantly to the diamond interest. Then he began to talk, in very Latin-Hebrew, helping out the sense now and again, where his vocabulary failed him, by waving his rather dirty and chemical-stained hands demonstratively about him. His nails were a sight, but his fingers, I must say, had the delicate shape of a man's accustomed to minute manipulation. He plunged at once into the thick of the matter, telling us briefly in his equally thick accent that he 'now proposed by his new process to make for us some good and satisfactory diamonds.'

He brought out his apparatus, and explained his novel method. 'Diamonds,' he said, 'were nothing but pure crystalline carbon. He knew how to crystallise it, that was all the secret.' The men of hermetic science examined the pots and pans carefully. Then he put in a certain number of raw materials, and went to work with ostentatious openness. There were three distinct processes, and he made two stones by each simultaneously. The remarkable part of his methods, he said, was their rapidity and their cheapness. In three-quarters of an hour (and he smiled sardonically) he could produce a diamond worth at current prices two hundred minas. 'As you shall now see me perform,' he remarked, 'with this simple apparatus.'

The materials fizzed and fumed. The alchemist stirred them. An unpleasant smell like burnt feathers pervaded the room. The occultists craned their necks in their eagerness, and looked over one another, After three-quarters of an hour, the hermeticist still smiling, began to empty the apparatus. He removed a large quantity of dust or powder, which he succinctly described as 'by-products,' and then took between finger and thumb from the midst of each pan a small white pebble, not water-worn apparently, but slightly rough and wart-like on the surface.

From one pair of the pannikins he produced two such stones, and held them up before us triumphantly. 'These,' he said, 'are genuine diamonds, manufactured at a cost of fourteen drachmas apiece!' Then he tried the second pair. 'These,' he said, still more gleefully, 'are produced at a cost of eleven drachmas!' Finally, he came to the third pair, which he positively brandished before our astonished eyes. 'And these,' he cried, transported, 'have cost me no more than four drachmas!'

They were handed round for inspection. Rough and uncut as they stood, it was, of course, impossible to judge of their value. But one thing was certain. The hermeticists had been watching close at the first, and were sure Sendivogius had not put the stones in, they were keen at the withdrawal, and were equally sure he had taken them honestly out of the pannikins.

'I will now distribute them,' the alchemist remarked in a casual tone, as if diamonds were peas, looking round at the company. And he singled out my brother-in-law. 'One to Judas!' he said, handing it out, 'one to Mr. Mosenheimer, one to Mr. Pilate, as representing the diamond interest. Then, one each to Atolphus, to Michael Maier, to Mr. Fane-Fiffian, as representing occult science. You will have them cut and report upon them in due course. We meet again at this place the day after tomorrow.'

Judas gazed at him reproachfully. The profoundest chords of his moral nature were stirred. 'Doctor alchemist,' he said, in a voice of solemn warning, 'are you aware that, if you have succeeded, you have destroyed the value of thousands of minas' worth of precious property?'

The hermeticist shrugged his shoulders. 'What is that to me?' he inquired, with a curious glance of contempt. 'I am not a camel dealer! I am a man steeped in ancient wisdom. I seek to know, I do not seek to make a fortune.'

'Shocking!' Judas exclaimed. 'Shocking! Never before in my life have I beheld so strange an instance of complete insensibility to the claims of others!'

We separated early. The occultists were coarsely jubilant. The diamond interest exhibited a corresponding depression. If this news were true, they foresaw a slump. Every eye grew dim. It was a terrible business. Judas walked homeward with the doctor alchemist. He sounded him gently as to the sum required, should need arise, to purchase his secrecy. Already Hermes had bound us all down to temporary silence, as if that were necessary, but Judas wished to know how much Sendivogius would take to suppress his discovery. The occultist was immovable.

'No, no!' he replied, with positive petulance. 'You do not understand. I do not buy and sell. This is an alchemical fact. We must publicise it for the sake off its mystical value. I do not care for wealth. I have no time to waste in making money.'

'What an awful picture of a misspent life!' Judas observed to me afterwards.

And, indeed, the man seemed to care for nothing on earth but occult questions, not whether he could make good diamonds or not, but whether he could or could not produce a crystalline form of pure carbon! On the appointed night Judas went back to Abraham's Gate, as I could not fail to remark, with a strange air of complete and painful preoccupation. Never before in his life had I seen him so anxious.

The diamonds were produced, with one surface of each slightly scored by the cutters, so as to show the water. Then a curious result disclosed itself. Strange to say, each of the three diamonds given to the three camel dealers turned out to be a most inferior and valueless stone, while each of the three entrusted to the care of the occult investigators turned out to be a fine gem of the purest quality.

I confess it was a sufficiently suspicious conjunction. The three representatives of the diamond interest gazed at each other with inquiring side-glances. Then their eyes fell suddenly: they avoided one another. Had each independently substituted a weak and inferior natural stone for Sendivogius's manufactured pebbles? It almost seemed so. For a moment, I admit, I was half inclined to suppose it. But next second I changed my mind. Could a man of Judas Iscariot's integrity and high principle stoop for lucre's sake to so mean an expedient? Not to mention the fact that, even if he did, and if Mosenheimer did likewise, the stones submitted to the occult men would have amply sufficed to establish the reality and success of the experiments! Still, I must say, Judas looked guiltily across at Mosenheimer, and Mosenheimer at Pilate, while three more uncomfortable or unhappy-faced men could hardly have been found at that precise minute in the Temple at Delphi.

Then Hermes spoke, or, rather, he orated. He said, in his loud and grating voice, we had that evening, and on a previous evening, been present at the conception and birth of an Epoch in the History of Occult Science. Michael Sendivogius was one of those men of whom his native Rome might well be proud, while as an Israelite he must say he regretted somewhat that this discovery, like so many others, should have been 'made in Rome.' However, Michael Sendivogius was a specimen of that noble type of alchemist to whom gold was merely the rare metal Au, and diamonds merely the element C in the scarcest of its manifold allotropic embodiments. The occult doctor did not seek to make money out of his discovery. He rose above the sordid greed of camel dealers. Content with the glory of having traced the element C to its crystalline origin, he asked no more than the approval of hermetic science. However, out of deference to the wishes of those camel dealing gentlemen who were oddly concerned in maintaining the present price of C in its crystalline form - in other words, the diamond interest - they had arranged that the secret should be strictly guarded and kept for the present, not one of the few persons admitted to the experiments would publicly divulge the truth about them. This secrecy would be maintained till he himself, and a small committee of kabalists, should have time to investigate and verify for themselves the occult doctor's beautiful and ingenious processes. An investigation and verification which the learned alchemist himself both desired and suggested. (Sendivogius nodded approval.) When that was done, if the process stood the test, further concealment would be absolutely futile. The price of diamonds must fall at once below that of paste, and any protest on the part of the camel dealing world would, of course, be useless. The laws of nature were superior to camel trading. Meanwhile, in deference to the opinion of Judas Iscariot, whose acquaintance with that fascinating side of the subject nobody could deny, they had consented to send no notices to their fellow occultists, and to abstain from saying anything about this beautiful and simple process in public. He dwelt with horrid gusto on that epithet 'beautiful.' And now, in the name of hermetic brotherhood, he must congratulate Doctor Sendivogius, our distinguished guest, on his truly brilliant and crystalline contribution to our knowledge of brilliants and of crystalline science.

Everybody applauded. It was an awkward moment. Judas bit his lip. Mosenheimer looked glum. Pilate dropped an expression which I cannot transcribe. And after a solemn promise of death-like secrecy, the meeting separated. I noticed that my brother-in-law somewhat ostentatiously avoided Mosenheimer at the door, and that Pilate jumped quickly onto his own camel. 'Home!' Judas cried gloomily. And all the way back his close-set lips never uttered a syllable. Before he retired to rest, however, in the privacy of the dice-room, I ventured to ask him: 'Judas, will you unload diamonds tomorrow?' Which, I need hardly explain, is slang for getting rid of undesirable assets. It struck me as probable that, in the event of the invention turning out a reality, our own diamond reserves might become unsaleable within the next few weeks or so.

He eyed me sternly. 'Christ,' he said, 'you're a fool!' (Except on occasions when he is very angry, my respected connection never calls me 'Christ', the familiar abbreviation,

'Jez' - derived from Jesus - is his usual mode of address to me in private.) 'Is it likely I would unload, and wreck the confidence of the public in diamonds at such a moment? Would it be just or right of me? I ask you, could I reconcile it to my conscience?'

'Judas,' I answered, 'you are right. Your conduct is noble. You will not save your own personal interests at the expense of those who have put their trust in you. Such probity is, alas, very rare in camel dealing!' And I sighed involuntarily, for I had recently lost money in the fig trade. At the same time I thought to myself, 'No trust is reposed in me. I have to think first of dear Mary and the baby. Before the crash comes I will sell out tomorrow the small stake I hold, through Judas's kindness, in precious stones.'

With his marvellous business instinct, Judas seemed to divine my thought, for he turned round to me sharply. 'Look here, Jez,' he remarked, in an acidulous tone, 'recollect, you're my brother-in-law. You are also my secretary. The eyes of Bethlehem will be upon us tomorrow. If you were to sell out, and operators got to know of it, they'd suspect there was something up, and every camel dealer would suffer for it. Of course, you can do what you like with your own property. I can't interfere with that. I do not dictate to you. But as the boss camel dealer, I am bound to see that the interests of my fellow camel dealers should not suffer at this crisis.' His voice seemed to falter. 'Therefore, though I don't like to threaten,' he went on, 'I am bound to give you warning: if you sell out those diamonds of yours, openly or secretly, you are no longer my secretary, you receive forthwith six months' salary in lieu of notice, and you leave me instantly.'

'Very well, Judas,' I answered, in a submissive voice, though I debated with myself for a moment whether it would be best to stick to the ready money and quit the sinking ship, or to hold fast by my friend, and back Judas's luck against occult science. After a short, sharp struggle within my own mind, I am proud to say, friendship and gratitude won. I felt sure that, whether diamonds went up or down, Judas Iscariot was the sort of man who would come to the top in the end in spite of everything. And I decided to stand by him!

I slept little that night, however. My mind was a whirlwind. At breakfast Judas also looked haggard and moody. He ordered the camels early, and rode straight to the bazaar.

There was a demonstration against camels being ridden through town going on near the Temple (their shit is allegedly a nuisance). Judas, impatient and nervous, tied up his camel and walked. I walked beside him. Near the bazaar a man we knew casually stopped us.

'I think I ought to mention to you,' he said, confidentially, 'that I have it on the very best authority that Sendivogius, of Rome...'

'Thank you,' Judas said, crustily, 'I know that tale, and there's not a word of truth in it.' He brushed on in haste. A yard or two farther a camel dealer paused in front of us.

'Hello, Judas!' he called out, in a bantering tone. 'What's all this about diamonds?'

Judas drew himself up very stiff. 'I fail to understand you,' he answered, with dignity.

'Why, you were there yourself,' the man cried. 'Last night at Hermes's! Oh yes, it's all over the place. Sendivogius of Rome has succeeded in making the most perfect diamonds for six leptons apiece. His diamonds are as good as real and camel dealing is ancient history. In less than six weeks Bethlehem and Nazareth, they say, will be a howling desert. Every slave will wear genuine Koh-i-noors for buttons on his coat, every girl will sport a riviere like Lady Iscariot's. There's a slump in diamonds. Sly, sly, I can see, but we know all about it!'

Judas moved on, disgusted. The man's manners were atrocious. Near the bazaar we ran up against a most respectable camel trader.

'Ah, Judas,' he said, 'you here? Well, this is strange news, isn't it? For my part, I advise you not to take it too seriously. Your diamonds will go down, of course, like lead this morning. But they'll rise tomorrow, mark my words, and fluctuate every hour till the discovery's proved or disproved for certain. There's a fine time coming for operators, I feel sure. Reports this way and that. Rumours, rumours, rumours. And nobody will know which way to jump till Hermes has tested it.'

We moved on towards the bazaar. Black care was seated on Judas's shoulders. As we drew nearer and nearer, everybody was discussing the one fact of the moment. The seal of secrecy had proved more potent than the story being shouted from the rooftops. Some people told us of the exciting news in confidential whispers, some proclaimed it aloud in vulgar exultation. The general opinion was that diamonds were doomed, and that the sooner a man cleared out the less was he likely to lose by it. Judas strode on like a general, but it was Caesar at the Ides of March. His mien was resolute. He disappeared at last into the precincts of the bazaar, waving me back, not to follow. After a long consultation he came out and rejoined me.

All day long the bazaar rang with diamonds, diamonds. Everybody murmured, 'Slump, slump in diamonds.' The camel dealers had more business to do than they could manage, though, to be sure, almost every one was a seller and no one a buyer. But Judas stood firm as a rock, and so did his partners. 'I don't want to sell,' he said, doggedly. 'The whole thing is trumped up. It's a mere piece of jugglery. For my own part, I believe Michael Sendivogius is deceived, or else is deceiving us. In another week the bubble will have burst, and prices will restore themselves.' Judas had every confidence in the stability of diamonds, and didn't wish to sell or to increase the panic.'

All the world said he was splendid, splendid! There he stationed himself like some granite stack against which the waves roll and break themselves in vain. He took no notice of the slump, but ostentatiously bought up a diamond here and there so as to restore public confidence.

'I would buy more,' he said, freely, 'and make my fortune, only, as I was one of those who happened to spend last night at Hermes's, people might think I had helped to spread the rumour and produce the slump, in order to buy in at panic rates for my own advantage. Like Ceasar's wife, I should be above suspicion. So I shall only buy up just enough, now and again, to let people see I, at least, have no doubt as to the firm future of diamonds.'

He went home that night, more harassed and ill than I have ever seen him. Next day was as bad. The slump continued, with varying episodes. Now, a rumour would surge up that Hermes had declared the whole affair a sham, and prices would steady a little, now, another would break out that the diamonds were actually being put upon the market by the cart-load, and timid old ladies would off-load their diamonds at whatever hazard. It was an awful day. I shall never forget it.

The morning after, as if by miracle, things righted themselves of a sudden. While we were wondering what it meant, Judas received a note from Hermes Trismegistus: 'The man is a fraud. Not Sendivogius at all. Just had a message from Rome saying the alchemist knows nothing about it. Sorry unintentionally to have caused you trouble. Come round and see me.'

Judas was beside himself with anger. Hermes had upset the trading at the bazaar for forty-eight mortal hours, half-ruined a round dozen of wealthy operators, convulsed the camel trade, upheaved Bethlehem, and now he apologised for it as one might apologise for being ten minutes late for dinner! Judas jumped onto a camel and rushed round to see him. How had he dared to introduce the impostor to solid men as Michael Sendivogius? Hermes shrugged his shoulders. The fellow had come and introduced himself as the great Roman alchemist, he had long white hair, and a stoop in the shoulders. What reason had he for doubting his word? (I reflected to myself that on much the same grounds Judas in turn had accepted David Baroni and Graf von Lebenstein.) Besides, what object could the creature have for this extraordinary deception? Judas knew only too well. It was clear it was done to disturb the diamond market, and we realised, too late, that the man who had done it was

Arugath ha-Bosem, in 'another of his manifold allotropic embodiments!' Judas had his wish, and had met his enemy once more in Bethlehem!

We could see the whole plot. Arugath ha-Bosem was polymorphic, like the element carbon! Doubtless, with his extraordinary sleight of hand, he had substituted real diamonds for the shapeless mass that came out of the apparatus, in the interval between handing the pebbles round for inspection, and distributing them piecemeal to the men of hermetic science and representatives of the diamond interest. We all watched him closely, of course, when he opened the crucibles, but when once we had satisfied ourselves that something came out, our doubts were set at rest, and we forgot to watch whether he distributed those somethings or not to the recipients. Conjurers always depend upon such momentary distractions or lapses of attention. As usual, too, the hermeticist had disappeared into space the moment his trick was once well performed. He vanished like smoke, as the Graf and Seer had vanished before, and was never heard of again.

Judas went home more angry than I have ever beheld him. I couldn't imagine why. He seemed as utterly fucked off as if he had lost his thousands. I endeavoured to console him. 'After all,' I said, 'though diamonds have suffered a temporary loss, it's a comfort to think that you should have stood so firm, and not only stemmed the tide, but also prevented yourself from losing anything at all of your own through panic. If Arugath ha-Bosem has rigged the market, at least it isn't you who lose by it this time.'

Judas withered me with a fierce scowl of undisguised contempt. 'Christ,' he said once more, 'you are a fool!' Then he relapsed into silence.

'But you declined to sell out,' I said.

He gazed at me fixedly. 'Is it likely,' he asked at last, 'I would tell you if I meant to sell out? or that I'd sell out openly? Why, all the world would have known, and diamonds would have been finished. As it is, I don't desire to tell an ass like you exactly how much I've lost. But I did sell out, and some unknown operator bought in at once, and closed for ready money, and has sold again this morning, and after all that has happened, it will be impossible to track him. He didn't wait for the account: he settled up instantly. And he sold in like manner. I know now what has been done, and how cleverly it has all been disguised and covered, but the most I'm going to tell you today is just this: it's by far the biggest haul Arugath ha-Bosem has made out of me. He could retire on it if he liked. My one hope is it may satisfy him for life, but, then, no man has ever had enough of making money.'

'You sold out!' I exclaimed. 'You deserted the ship!'

Judas rose and faced me. 'Jesus H. Christ,' he said, in his most solemn voice, 'you have lived with me for years and had every advantage. You have seen camel dealing. Yet you express surprise and indignation! It's my belief you will never, never understand business!'

CHAPTER TWELVE

Shortly after this incident with the diamonds, the wife of a merchant who was transacting some business with Judas came to stay with us. She was offered as security until the deal being cut could be completed to the satisfaction of both parties involved. However, when the merchant in question absconded with forty camels and many valuables, cursory enquiries brought the news that the man concerned cared little for his wife and his long-standing mistreatment of her was common gossip in their home town. However, the woman's tearful litany of the indignities she'd suffered at her husband's hands did little to soften the enmity Judas felt towards her - and he ordered me to ravish the jade as we'd originally planned if things went wrong. She had a room of her own and was in the habit of locking herself in it when she retired for the night. So I stripped naked one evening after supper and hid myself behind the woman's bed. Your can imagine the wronged wife's terror when I sprang up after she'd bolted herself into the room and was in the process of removing her robes.

Defenceless and naked in my arms, I carried the merchant's wife to the bed and threw her down upon it. Her shrieks could be heard in the street but no one paid the least heed to them. What could the feeble wife of a swindler effect against so powerful an antagonist as Judas Iscariot. Since the woman's chastity had long before been reduced to a bleeding ruin, she quickly found it was useless to struggle or resist my actions. Though a mature woman, she was a mere child in my arms. I moved and placed her as was convenient to my pleasure. I felt myself harden and used a hand to introduce my manhood to her inner sanctuary.

Directly I had loaded my cock into the jade, I withdrew my hands and placed my arms around her neck. I drew her lips to mine. So overcome by fear and shame was the merchant's wife, that she made no motion to resist me. But as I forced my way deeper inside, she was roused to indignation. She screamed with anguish but her petitions, supplications and tears were no use. She was my altar and I was determined to complete the sacrifice. Indeed, her cries served only to excite me and sealed her ruin. Soon my shaft was buried to its hilt within her, resulting in the copious flow of unctuous streams of steaming spunk. Having had my way with the abandoned wife, I dressed and drove her naked into the street, as Judas had instructed. How she made her way in the world from this juncture was of no concern to my master.

CHAPTER THIRTEEN

How much precisely Judas dropped over the slump in diamonds I never quite knew. But the incident left him dejected, limp, and dispirited.

'Hang it all, Jez,' he said to me in the dice-room a few evenings later. 'This Arugath ha-Bosem is enough to vex the patience of Job, and Job had large losses, too, if I recollect aright, from the Chaldeans and other big operators of the period.'

'Three thousand camels,' I murmured, recalling my dear mother's lessons, 'all at one fell swoop, not to mention five hundred yoke of oxen, carried off by the Sabeans, then a leading firm of speculative cattle-dealers!'

'Ah, well,' Judas meditated aloud, shaking the ash from the banana skin he was smoking onto the floor. 'There were big transactions in live-stock even then! Still, Job or no Job, the man is too much for me.'

'The difficulty is,' I assented, 'you never know where to look out for him.'

'Yes,' Judas mused, 'if he were always the same, like an old whore or a confirmed piss-head, it would be easier, of course, you'd stand some chance of spotting him. But when a man turns up smiling every time in a different disguise, which fits him like a skin, and always apparently with the best credentials, why, hang it all, Jez, there's no wrestling with him anyhow.'

'Who could have come to us, for example, better vouched,' I acquiesced,' than David Baroni?'

'Exactly so,' Judas murmured. 'I invited him myself, for my own advantage. And he arrived with all the prestige of the Jericho connection.'

'Or the gem-making alchemist?' I went on. 'Introduced to us by the leading occultist of our land.'

I had touched a sore point. Judas winced and remained

silent.

'Then, women again,' he resumed, after a painful pause. 'I must meet in society many charming women. I can't everywhere and always be on my guard against every last one of them. Yet the moment I relax my attention for one day - or even when I don't relax it - I am bamboozled and led a dance by that arch Mme. Picardet, or that transparently simple little minx, Mrs. Baroni. She's the cleverest girl I ever met in my life, that hussy, whatever we're to call her. She's a different person each time, and each time, hang it all, I lose my heart afresh to that different person.'

I glanced round to make sure Martha was well out of earshot.

'No, Jez,' my respected connection went on, after another long pause, sipping his sweet wine pensively, 'I feel I must be aided in this superhuman task by a professional unraveller of cunning disguises. I shall go to Al-Hazred's tomorrow - fortunate man, Al-Hazred - and ask him to supply me with a really good detective, who will stop in the house and keep an eye upon every living soul that comes near me. He shall scan each nose, each eye, each wig, each whisker. He shall be my watchful half, my unsleeping self, it shall be his business to suspect all living men, all breathing women. The Chief Rabbi of Jerusalem shall not escape for a moment his watchful regard. He will take care that royal princesses don't collar the spoons or walk off with the jewel-cases. He must see possible Arugath ha-Bosems in the guard of every camel pack and the rabbi of every synagogue, he must detect the off-chance of a Mme. Picardet in every young girl that takes tea with Martha, every fat old lady that comes to call upon Mary. Yes, I have made my mind up. I shall go tomorrow and secure such a man at once at Al-Hazred's.'

'If you please, Judas,' Cesarine interposed, pushing her head through the portiere, 'her ladyship says, will you and Mr. Christ remember that she goes out with you both this evening to Sophia Torah's?'

'Bless my soul,' Judas cried, 'so she does! And it's now past ten! The camels will be at the door for us in another five minutes!'

Next morning, accordingly, Judas rode round to Al-Hazred's. The famous detective listened to his story with glistening eyes, then he rubbed his hands and purred. 'Arugath ha-Bosem!' he said, 'Arugath ha-Bosem! That's a very tough customer! The police of the entire Roman Empire are on the look-out for Arugath ha-Bosem. He is wanted in Bethlehem, in Naples, in Rome. It is le Arugath Caoutchouc here, le Arugath Caoutchouc there, till one begins to ask, at last, is there one Arugath Caoutchouc, or is it a convenient class name invented by the Force to cover a gang of undiscovered sharpers? However, Judas, we will do our best. I will set on the track without delay the best and cleverest detective in the Roman Empire.'

'The very man I want,' Judas said. 'What name, Al-Hazred?'

The principal smiled. 'Whatever name you like,' he said. 'He isn't particular. Eleazer of Worms he's called at home. We call him The Golem. I'll send him round to your house this afternoon for certain.'

'Oh no,' Judas said promptly, 'you won't, or Arugath ha-Bosem himself will come instead of him. I've been sold too often. No casual strangers! I'll wait here and see him.'

'But he isn't in,' Al-Hazred objected.

Judas was firm as a rock. 'Then send and fetch him.'

In half an hour, sure enough, the detective arrived. He was an odd-looking small man, with hair cut short and standing straight up all over his head, like a hick waiter from Gaul. He had quick, sharp eyes, very much like a ferret's, his nose was depressed, his lips thin and bloodless. A scar marked his left cheek. He said it was made by a sword-cut he received while arresting a desperate Gaulish smuggler, disguised as an officer of Chasseurs d'Afrique. His mien was resolute. Altogether, a quainter or cuter little man it has never yet been my lot to set eyes on. He walked in with a brisk step, eyed Judas up and down, and then, without much formality, asked for what he was wanted.

This is Judas Iscariot, the great camel trader,' Al-Hazred said, introducing us.

'So I see,' the man answered.

'Then you know me?' Judas asked.

'I wouldn't be worth much,' the detective replied, 'if I didn't know everybody. And you're easy enough to know, why, every whore in town knows you and most have fucked you more than once.'

'Plain spoken!' Judas remarked.

'As you like it,' the man answered in a respectful tone. 'I endeavour to suit my dress and behaviour on every occasion to the taste of my employers.'

'Your name?' Judas asked, smiling.

'Golem Eleazer of Worms, at your service. What sort of work? Stolen camels? Illicit sex with young boys?'

'No,' Judas answered, fixing him with his eye. 'Quite another kind of job. You've heard of Arugath ha-Bosem?'

Eleazer of Worms nodded. 'Why, certainly,' he said, and, for the first time, I detected a lingering trace of a Latin accent. 'It's my business to know about him.'

'Well, I want you to catch him,' Judas went on.

Eleazer of Worms drew a long breath. 'Isn't that rather a tall order?' he murmured, surprised.

Judas explained to him exactly the sort of services he required. Eleazer of Worms promised to comply. 'If the man comes near you, I'll spot him,' he said, after a moment's pause. 'I can promise you that much. I'll pierce any disguise. I should know in a minute whether he's got up or not. I'm death on wigs, false moustaches, artificial complexions. I'll engage to bring the rogue to book if I see him. You may set your mind at rest, that, while I'm about you, Arugath ha-Bosem can do nothing without my instantly spotting him.'

'He'll do it,' Al-Hazred put in. 'He'll do it, if he says it. He's my very best hand. Never knew any man like him for unravelling and unmasking the cleverest disguises.'

'Then he'll suit me,' Judas answered, 'for I never knew any man like Arugath ha-Bosem for assuming and maintaining them.'

It was arranged accordingly that Eleazer of Worms should take up his residence in the house for the present, and should be described to the servants as assistant secretary. He came that very day, with a marvellously small portmanteau. But from the moment he arrived, we noticed that Cesarine took a violent dislike to him.

Eleazer of Worms was a most efficient detective. Judas and I told him all we knew about the various shapes in which Arugath ha-Bosem had 'materialised,' and he gave us in turn many valuable criticisms and suggestions. Why, when we began to suspect David Baroni, had we not, as if by accident, tried to knock his red wig off? Why, when the Reverend Isaac Adam Brabazon first discussed the question of the paste diamonds, had we not looked to see if any of Martha's unique gems were missing? Why, when the alchemist Sendivogius made his bow to assembled occult science at Abraham's Gate, had we not strictly inquired how far he was personally known beforehand to Hermes Trismegistus and the other kabalists? He supplied us also with several good hints about false hair and make-up, such as that Sendivogius was probably much shorter than he looked, but by imitating a stoop with padding at his back he had produced the illusion of a tall bent man, though in reality no bigger than the little rabbi or the Graf von Lebenstein. High heels did the rest, while the scientific keenness we noted in his face was doubtless brought about by a trifle of wax at the end of the nose, giving a peculiar tilt that is extremely effective. In short, I must frankly admit, Eleazer of Worms made us feel ashamed of ourselves. Sharp as Judas is, we realised at once he was nowhere in observation beside the trained and experienced senses of this professional detective.

The worst of it all was, while Eleazer of Worms was with us, by some curious fatality, Arugath ha-Bosem stopped away from us. Now and again, to be sure, we ran up against somebody whom Eleazer of Worms suspected, but after a short investigation (conducted, I may say, with admirable cleverness), the spy always showed us the doubtful person was really some innocent and well-known character, whose antecedents and surroundings he elucidated most wonderfully. He was a perfect marvel, too, in his faculty of suspicion. He suspected everybody. If an old friend dropped in to talk business with Judas, we found out afterwards that Eleazer of Worms had lain concealed all the time behind the curtain, and had taken notes of the whole conversation, as well as impressions of the supposed sharper, by means of papyrus and a charcoal stick. If a fat old lady came to call upon Martha, Eleazer of Worms was sure to be lurking under the ottoman in the drawing-room, and carefully observing, with all his eyes, whether or not she was really Mme. Picardet, padded. When Lady Tresco brought her four plain daughters to an 'At Home' one night, Eleazer of Worms, in evening robes, disguised as a waiter, followed them each round the room with obtrusive ices, to satisfy himself just how much of their complexion was real, and how much was patent rouge and Bloom of Ninon. He suspected Judas's valet slave was Arugath ha-Bosem in plain clothes, and he had half an idea that Cesarine herself was our saucy Supreme Crown in disguise. We pointed out to him in vain that the valet had often been present in the very same room with David Baroni, and that Cesarine had dressed Mrs. Brabazon's hair at Amman: this partially satisfied him, but only partially. He remarked that the valet might double both parts with somebody else unknown, and that as for Cesarine, she might well have a twin sister who took her place when she was Mme. Picardet.

Still, in spite of all his care - or because of all his care - Arugath ha-Bosem stopped away for whole weeks together. An explanation occurred to us. Was it possible he knew we were guarded and watched? Was he afraid of measuring swords with this trained detective?

If so, how had he found it out? I had an inkling but,

under all the circumstances, I did not mention it to Judas. It was clear that Cesarine intensely disliked this new addition to the Iscariot household. She would not stop in the room where the detective was, or show him common politeness. She spoke of him always as 'that odious man, Eleazer of Worms.' Could she have guessed, what none of the other servants knew, that the man was a spy in search of Arugath? I was inclined to believe it. And then it dawned upon me that Cesarine had known all about the diamonds and their story, that it was Cesarine who took us to see Schloss Lebenstein, that it was Cesarine who carried the letter to Pontius Pilate! If Cesarine was in league with Arugath ha-Bosem, as I was half inclined to surmise, what more natural than her obvious dislike of the detective who was there to catch her principal? What more simple for her than to warn her fellow conspirator of the danger that awaited him if he approached this man Eleazer of Worms? However, I was too much frightened by the episode of the cheque to say anything of my nascent suspicions to Judas. I waited rather to see how events would shape themselves.

After a while Eleazer of Worms's vigilance grew positively annoying. More than once he came to Judas with reports and notes distinctly distasteful to my excellent brother-in-law. 'He raised suspicions about the madam of a brothel that I have patronised for years. The fellow is getting to know too much about us,' Judas said to me one day. 'Why, Jez, he spies out everything. Would you believe it, when I had that confidential interview with Pitchon the other day, about the new trading practices of using diamonds rather than coins for big transactions, the man was under the easy-chair, though I searched the room beforehand to make sure he wasn't there. He came to me afterwards with full notes of the conversation, to assure me he thought Pitchon - whom I've known for ten years - was too tall by half an inch to be one of Arugath ha-Bosem's impersonations.'

'Oh, but, Judas,' Eleazer of Worms cried, emerging suddenly from behind a door, 'you must never look upon anyone as above suspicion merely because you've known him for ten years or thereabouts. Arugath ha-Bosem may have approached you at various times under many disguises. He may have built up this thing gradually. Besides, as to my knowing too much, why, of course, a detective always learns many things about his employer's family which he is not supposed to know. However, professional honour and professional etiquette, as with kabalists and scribes, compel him to lock them up as absolute secrets in his own bosom. You need never be afraid I will divulge one jot of them. If I did, my occupation would be gone, and my reputation shattered.'

Judas looked at him, appalled. 'Do you dare to say,' he burst out, 'you've been listening to my talk with my brother-in-law and secretary?'

'Why, of course,' Eleazer of Worms answered. 'It's my business to listen, and to suspect everybody. If you push me to say so, how do I know Arugath ha-Bosem is not Mr. Christ?'

Judas withered him with a look. 'In future, Eleazer of Worms,' he said, 'you must never conceal yourself in a room where I am without my leave and knowledge.'

Eleazer of Worms bowed politely. 'Oh, as you will, Judas,' he answered, 'that's quite at your own wish. Though how can I act as an efficient detective, anyway, if you insist upon tying my hands like that, beforehand?'

Again I detected a faint Latin flavour. After that rebuff, however, Eleazer of Worms seemed put upon his mettle. He redoubled his vigilance in every direction. 'It's not my fault,' he said plaintively, one day, 'if my reputation's so good that, while I'm near you, this rogue won't approach you. If I can't catch him, at least I keep him from coming near you!'

A few days later, however, he brought Judas some charcoal drawings. These he produced with evident pride. The first he showed us was a vignette of a little rabbi. 'Who's that, then?' he inquired, much pleased.

We gazed at it, open-eyed. One word rose to our lips simultaneously: 'Brabazon!'

'And how's this for likeness?' he asked producing another, a drawing of a gay young dog in a Tyrolese costume.

We murmured, 'Von Lebenstein!'

'And this?' he continued, showing us a portrait of a lady with a most fetching squint.

We answered with one voice, 'Little Mrs. Baroni!'

Eleazer of Worms was naturally proud of this excellent exploit. He replaced them in his pocket-book with an air of just triumph.

'How did you get them?' Judas asked.

Eleazer of Worms's look was mysterious. 'Judas,' he answered, drawing himself up, 'I must ask you to trust me awhile in this matter. Remember, there are people whom you decline to suspect. I have learned that it is always those very people who are most dangerous to camel dealers. If I were to give you the names now, you would refuse to believe me. Therefore, I hold them over discreetly for the moment. One thing, however, I say. I know to a certainty where Arugath ha-Bosem is right now. But I will lay my plans deep, and I hope before long to secure him. You shall be present when I do so and I shall make him confess his personality openly. More than that you cannot reasonably ask. I shall leave it to you, then, whether or not you wish to arrest him.'

Judas was considerably puzzled, not to say piqued, by this curious reticence, he begged hard for names, but Eleazer of Worms was adamant. 'No, no,' he replied, 'we detectives have our own just pride in our profession. If I told you now, you would probably spoil all by some premature action. You are too open and impulsive! I will mention this alone: Arugath ha-Bosem will be shortly in Jerusalem, and before long will begin from that city a fresh attempt at defrauding you, which he is now hatching. Mark my words, and see whether or not I have been kept well informed of the fellow's movements!'

He was perfectly correct. Two days later, as it turned out, Judas received a 'confidential' letter from Jerusalem, purporting to come from the head of a second-rate camel dealership with which he'd had dealings over the Pontius Pilate Amalgamation - by this time, I ought to have said, an accomplished union. It was a letter of small importance in itself, a mere matter of detail, but Eleazer of Worms insisted it paved the way to some later development of more serious character. Here once more the man's singular foresight was justified. For, in another week, we received a second communication, containing other proposals of a delicate financial character, which would have involved the transference of some two thousand minas to the head of the Jerusalem firm at an address given. Both these letters Eleazer of Worms cleverly compared with those written to Judas before, in the names of Arugath ha-Bosem and Graf von Lebenstein. At first sight, it is true, the differences between the two seemed quite enormous: the Jerusalem hand was broad and black, large and bold, while the earlier manuscript was small, neat, thin, and gentlemanly. Still, when Eleazer of Worms pointed out to us certain persistent twists in the formation of his capitals, and certain curious peculiarities in the relative length of his t's, his i's, his b's, and his h's, we could see for ourselves he was right, both were the work of one hand, writing in the one case with a sharp-pointed quill, very small, and in the other with a blunt quill, very large and freely.

This discovery was most important. We stood now within measurable distance of catching Arugath ha-Bosem, and bringing forgery and fraud home to him without hope of evasion. To make all sure, however, Eleazer of Worms communicated with the Jerusalem police, and showed us their answers. Meanwhile, Judas continued to write to the head of the firm, who had given a private address, alleging, I must say, a most clever reason why the negotiations at this stage should be confidentially conducted. But one never expected from Arugath ha-Bosem anything less than consummate cleverness. In the end, it was arranged that we three were to go over to Jerusalem together, that Eleazer of Worms was to undertake, under the guise of being Judas, to pay the two thousand minas to the pretended financier, and that Judas and I, waiting with the police outside the door, should, at a given signal, rush in with our forces and secure the criminal.

We went over accordingly, and spent the night at the Cain & Abel, as is Judas's custom. The Naked Eve, which I prefer, he finds too quiet. Early next morning we rode across town. Eleazer of Worms had arranged everything in advance with the Jerusalem police, three of whom, in plain clothes, were waiting at the foot of the staircase to assist us. Judas had further provided himself with two thousand minas, in talent coins, in order that the payment might be duly made, and no doubt arise as to the crime having been perpetrated as well as meditated. In the former case, the penalty would be crucifixion (assuming, of course, our enemy was not a Roman citizen, if he was he would be beheaded), in the latter case, the penalty was the mere loss of a hand. Judas was in very high spirits. The fact that we had tracked the rascal to earth at last, and were within an hour of apprehending him, was in itself enough to raise his courage greatly. We found, as we expected, that the address given was that of an inn, not a private residence. Eleazer of Worms went in first, and inquired of the landlord whether our man was at home, at the same time informing him of the nature of our errand, and giving him to understand that if we effected the capture by his friendly aid, Judas would see that the expenses incurred on the swindler's bill were met in full, as the price of his assistance. The landlord bowed, he expressed his deep regret, as Arugath was a most amiable person, much liked by the household, but justice, of course, must have its way, and, with a regretful sigh, he undertook to assist us.

The police remained below, but Judas and Eleazer of Worms were each provided with a stout rope. Remembering the Ben Shesheth case, however, we determined to use the restraints with the greatest caution. We would only use them in case of violent resistance. We crept up to the door where the miscreant was housed. Judas handed the coins to Eleazer of Worms, who seized them hastily and held them in his hands in readiness for action. Whenever he sneezed - which he could do in the most natural manner - we were to open the door, rush in, and secure the criminal!

He was gone for some minutes. Judas and I waited outside in breathless expectation. Then Eleazer of Worms sneezed. We flung the door open at once, and burst in upon the creature.

Eleazer of Worms rose as we did so. He pointed with his finger. 'This is Arugath ha-Bosem!' he said, 'keep him well in charge while I go down to the door for the police to arrest him!'

A gentlemanly man, about middle height, with a grizzled beard and a well-assumed military aspect, rose at the same moment. 'I am at a loss, gentlemen,' he said, in an excited voice, 'to account for this interruption.' He spoke with a tremor, yet with all the politeness to which we were accustomed in the little rabbi and David Baroni.

'No, nonsense!' Judas exclaimed in his authoritative way. 'We know who you are. We have found you out this time. You are Arugath ha-Bosem. If you attempt to resist, take care, I will bind you!'

The military gentleman gave a start. 'Yes, I am Arugath ha-Bosem,' he answered. 'On what charge do you arrest me?'

Judas was bursting with wrath. The fellow's coolness seemed never to desert him. 'You are Arugath ha-Bosem!' he muttered. 'You have the unspeakable effrontery to stand there and admit it?'

'Certainly,' Arugath answered, growing hot in turn. 'I have done nothing to be ashamed of. What do you mean by this conduct? How dare you talk of arresting me?'

Judas laid his hand on the man's shoulder. 'Come, come, my friend,' he said. 'That sort of bluff won't go down with us. You know very well on what charge I arrest you, and here are the police to give effect to it.'

He called out 'Entrez!' The police entered the room. Judas explained what they were to do next. Arugath drew himself up in an indignant attitude. He turned and addressed them.

'I am an officer in the service of the Roman Emperor,' he said. 'On what ground do you venture to interfere with me?'

The chief policeman explained. Arugath turned to Judas. 'Your name?' he inquired.

'You know it very well,' Judas answered. 'I am Judas Iscariot, and, in spite of your clever disguise, I can instantly recognise you. I know your eyes and ears. I can see the same man who cheated me at Naples, and who insulted me on the island.'

'You Judas Iscariot!' the rogue cried. 'No, no, you are a madman!' He looked round at the police. 'Take care what you do!' he cried. 'This is a raving maniac. I had business just now with Judas Iscariot, who quitted the room as these gentlemen entered. This person is mad, and you, sir, I doubt not,' bowing to me, 'you are, of course, his keeper.'

'Do not let him deceive you,' I cried to the police, beginning to fear that with his usual incredible cleverness the fellow would even now manage to slip through our fingers. 'Arrest him, as you are told. We will take the responsibility.' Though I trembled when I thought of that cheque he held of mine.

The chief of our three policemen came forward and laid his hand on the culprit's shoulder. 'I advise you, Arugath,' he said, in an official voice, 'to come with us quietly for the present. Before the scribe we can enter at length into all these questions.'

Arugath, very indignant still and acting the part marvellously, yielded and went along with them.

'Where's Eleazer of Worms?' Judas inquired, glancing round as we reached the door. 'I wish he had stopped with us.'

'You are looking for your friend?' the landlord inquired, with a side bow to Arugath. 'He has gone away on a camel. He asked me to give you this note.'

He handed us a twisted papyrus. Judas opened and read it. 'Invaluable man!' he cried. 'Just hear what he says, Jez: 'Having secured Arugath ha-Bosem, I am off now again on the track of Mme. Picardet. She was lodging in the same house. She has just driven away, I know to what place, and I am after her to arrest her. In blind haste, ELEAZER OF WORMS.' That's smartness, if you like. Though poor little woman, I think he might have left her.'

'Does a Mme. Picardet stop here?' I inquired of the landlord, thinking it possible she might have assumed again the same old alias.

He nodded assent. 'Yes, yes, yes,' he answered. 'She has just ridden off on a camel, and your friend has gone posting after her.'

'Splendid man!' Judas cried. 'Al-Hazred was quite right. He is the prince of detectives!'

We mounted our camels and rode off to the scribe. There Arugath ha-Bosem continued to brazen it out, and asserted that he was an officer in the Roman Army, home on six months' leave, and spending some weeks in Jerusalem. He even declared he was known at the Greek Embassy, where he had a cousin, an attaché, and he asked that this gentleman should be sent for at once from the Ambassador's to identify him. The scribe insisted that this must be done, and Judas waited in very bad humour for the foolish formality. It really seemed as if, after all, when we had actually caught and arrested our man, he was going by some cunning device to escape us.

After a delay of more than an hour, during which Arugath ha-Bosem fretted and fumed quite as much as we did, the attaché arrived. To our horror and astonishment, he proceeded to salute the prisoner most affectionately.

'Hello, Algy!' he cried, grasping his hand, what's up? What do these ruffians want with you?'

It began to dawn upon us, then, what Eleazer of Worms had meant by 'suspecting everybody': the real Arugath ha-Bosem was no common adventurer, but a gentleman of birth and high connections!

Arugath glared at us. 'This fellow declares he's Judas Iscariot,' he said sulkily. 'Though, in fact, there are two of them. And he accuses me of forgery, fraud, and theft, Zeus.'

The attaché stared hard at us. 'This is Judas Iscariot,' he replied, after a moment. 'I remember hearing him make a speech once at a dinner. And what charge have you to prefer, Judas, against my cousin?'

'Your cousin?' Judas cried. 'This is Arugath ha-Bosem, the notorious sharper!'

The attaché smiled a gentlemanly and superior smile. 'This is Arugath ha-Bosem,' he answered, 'of the First Roman Legion.'

It began to strike us there was something wrong somewhere.

'But he has cheated me, all the same,' Judas said, 'at Naples two years ago, and many times since, and this very day he has tricked me out of two thousand minas in coins, which he has now about him!'

Arugath was speechless. But the attaché laughed. 'What he has done today I don't know,' he said, 'but if it's as apocryphal as what you say he did two years ago, you've a thundering bad case, for he was then in Gaul, and I was out there, visiting him.'

'Where are the two thousand minas?' Judas cried. 'Why, you've got them in your pockets, which are bulging!'

Arugath produced them. 'This money,' he said, 'was left with me by the man with short stiff hair, who came just before you, and who announced himself as Judas Iscariot. He said he was interested in importing tea from Assam, and wanted me to join his partnership.'

'Well, I'm glad the money is safe, anyhow,' Judas murmured, in a tone of relief, beginning to smell a rat. 'Will you kindly return it to me?'

The innocent man turned out the contents of his pockets. The cash was widow's mites, low value copper coins, not talents, which are of the highest value.

'Eleazer of Worms must have put them there,' I cried, 'and decamped with the cash.'

Judas gave a groan of horror. 'And Eleazer of Worms is

Arugath ha-Bosem!' he exclaimed, clapping his hand to his forehead.

'I beg your pardon,' Arugath interposed. 'I have but one personality, and no aliases.'

It took quite half an hour to unravel this imbroglio. But as soon as everything was explained to the satisfaction of the scribe, the real Arugath shook hands with us in a most forgiving way, and informed us that he had more than once wondered, when he gave his name at shops in Jerusalem, why it was often received with such grave suspicion. We instructed the police that the true culprit was Eleazer of Worms, whom they had seen with their own eyes, and whom we urged them to pursue with all expedition. Meanwhile, Judas and I, accompanied by Arugath and the attaché - 'to see the fun out,' as they said - returned to the inn. We learnt from the inn-keeper that Mme. Picardet had taken rooms in the same inn, to be near the soldier Arugath, and it was she who had received and sent the letters. As for our foe, he had vanished into space, as always.

Two days later we received the usual insulting communication on a sheet of Judas's own top quality papyrus. Last time he wrote it was on Pontius Pilate's papyrus: this time, like the wanton lapwing, he had got himself another crest: 'MOST PERSPICACIOUS OF CAMEL DEALERS! Said I not well, as Eleazer of Worms, that you must distrust everybody? And the one man you never dreamt of distrusting was Eleazer of Worms. Yet see how truthful I was! I told you I knew where Arugath ha-Bosem was living - and I did know, exactly. I promised to take you to Arugath ha-Bosem's rooms, and to get him arrested for you - and I kept my promise. I even exceeded your expectations, for I gave you two Arugath ha-Bosems instead of one - and you took the wrong man - that is to say, the real one. This was a neat little trick, but it cost me some trouble.

'First, I found out there was a real Arugath ha-Bosem, in the Roman Army. I also found out he chanced to be coming home on leave this season. I might have made more out of him, no doubt, but I disliked annoying him, and preferred to give myself the fun of this peculiar mystification. I therefore waited for him to reach Jerusalem, where the police arrangements suited me better than in Bethlehem. While I was looking about, and delaying operations for his return, I happened to hear you wanted a detective. So I offered myself as out of work to my old employer, Al-Hazred, from whom I have had many good jobs in the past, and there you get, in short, the kernel of Arugath.

'Naturally, after this, I can never go back as a detective to Al-Hazred's. But, on the large scale on which I have learned to work since I first had the pleasure of making your delightful acquaintance, this matters little. To tell the truth, I begin to feel detective work a cut or two below me. I am now a gentleman of means and leisure. Besides, the extra knowledge of your movements which I have acquired in your house has helped still further to give me various holds upon you. So the fluke will be true to his own pet lamb. To vary the metaphor, you are not fully shorn yet.

'Remember me most kindly to your charming family, give Christ my love, and tell Cesarine I owe her a grudge which I shall never forget. She clearly suspected me. You are much too rich, dear Judas, I relieve your plethora. I bleed you financially. Therefore I consider myself, your sincerest friend, 'HA-BOSEM-BRABAZON-ELEAZER OF WORMS, Fellow of the Invisible College.'

Judas was threatened with apoplexy. This blow was severe. 'Whom can I trust,' he asked, plaintively, 'when the detectives themselves, whom I employ to guard me, turn out to be swindlers? Don't you remember that line in the Latin grammar, something about, 'Who shall watch the watchers?' I think it runs, 'Quis custodes custodiet ipsos?' But I felt this episode had at least disproved my suspicions of poor Cesarine.

CHAPTER FOURTEEN

Around this time, Judas was suffering from sexual exhaustion, and unable to fuck would have me accompany him to a brothel where he would watch me in action with the whores. The first time he ordered a virgin to be stripped naked and once this task was accomplished, he dismissed the eunuchs who'd carried out his instructions. They retired taking away the newly enslaved virgin's clothes. So much were the maiden's feelings overcome that she felt obliged to seat herself on the very couch that had been provided for my pleasure. In a few seconds I stripped myself naked and took the woman in my arms. After kissing her, I told her I had come to redress the cruel wrongs she had suffered since her capture. When she was about to experience love for the first time since her abduction from her native soil, I asked her why she cried? I told her I would have no more of her folly, and Judas applauded as I drew her to my breast.

I ordered the maiden to open her soft thighs, telling her that she must lie on her back to receive my warm benedictions. The woman dared not disobey me and in an instant I was between her legs. The slave looked unhappy, so I tried to soothe her with endearments, telling her the pain would be nothing and the pleasures that followed it worth the whole world. Her fears were unfounded, it was a sacrifice that nature had decreed and Judas had paid for. The sweetest joys were to be her reward, so we would have no more of foolish fears. Thus did I soften the virgin to my desires and the head of my instrument was no sooner fixed to her opening than by four or five sudden shoves, I contrived to insert the whole of it entirely. At that moment my penetration was not deep enough to make the maiden experience any great pain, but well knowing what was coming, I forcibly secured one of my arms around her body.

Everything was thus prepared and favourable. Her legs were glued to mine, and she lay in my arms as it were insensible from despair, shame and confusion. I improved my advantage by forcibly deepening my penetration. My prodigious stiffness and size gave the woman a dreadful anguish from the separation of the sides of her soft passage by such a hard substance, that she could not refrain from screaming, a turn of events that caused Judas to laugh heartily. Delicate as she was, I found the maiden's resistance hard to overcome, but my Herculean belief in patriarchy and the male principle broke down all her virgin defences. Her piercing screams spoke of her sufferings and gave Judas great joy. The woman strove to escape, but perfectly used to such attempts I easily foiled them with my able thrusts, and I quickly buried my instrument too far within her to leave any chance of escape.

I paid no attention to her sufferings, but followed up my movements with fury, and the tender texture of my earlier coaxing gave way to fierce tearing and rending, and one merciless, violent thrust broke in and carried all before it, sending my weapon, imbued and reeking with the blood of her virginity, up to its utmost length in her body. The piercing shriek she gave proclaimed that she felt it up to the very quick, in short my victory was complete. Judas said nothing but clapped and laughed. There wasn't any need for words. There was an unspoken understanding between us about the ways in which God had ordained through his rendering of nature that men should assert their mastery over women.

CHAPTER FIFTEEN

On our return to Bethlehem, Judas and Al-Hazred had a difference of opinion on the subject of Eleazer of Worms. Judas maintained that Al-Hazred ought to have known the man with the cropped hair was Arugath ha-Bosem, and ought never to have recommended him. Al-Hazred maintained that Judas had seen Arugath ha-Bosem half-a-dozen times, at least, to his own never, and that my respected brother-in-law had therefore nobody on earth but himself to blame if the rogue imposed upon him. The head detective had known Eleazer of Worms for ten years, he said, as a most respectable man, and even a ratepayer, he had always found him the cleverest of spies, as well he might be, indeed, on the familiar set-a-thief-to-catch-a-thief principle. However, the upshot of it all was, as usual nothing. Al-Hazred was sorry to lose the services of so excellent a hand, but he had done the very best he could for Judas, he declared, and if Judas was not satisfied, why, he might catch his Arugath ha-Bosems for himself in future.

'So I will, Jez,' Judas remarked to me, as we walked back from the bazaar. 'I won't trust any more to these private detectives. It's my belief they're a pack of thieves themselves, in league with the rascals they're set to catch, and with no more sense of honour than an ordinary camel-hand.'

'Better try the police,' I suggested, by way of being helpful. One must assume an interest in one's employer's business.

But Judas shook his head. 'No, no,' he said, 'I'm sick of all these fellows. I shall trust in future to my own sagacity. We learn by experience, Jez and I've learned a thing or two. One of them is this: it's not enough to suspect everybody, you must have no preconceptions. Divest yourself entirely of every fixed idea if you wish to cope with a rascal of this calibre. Don't jump at conclusions. We should disbelieve everything, as well as distrust everybody. That's the road to success, and I mean to pursue it.'

So, by way of pursuing it, Judas retired to Nazareth.

'The longer the man goes on, the worse he grows,' he said to me one morning. 'He's just like a tiger that has tasted blood. Every successful haul seems only to make him more eager for another. I fully expect now before long we shall see him down here.'

About three weeks later, sure enough, my respected connection received a communication from the swindler, carrying a Roman stamp and a Pisa post-mark.

'MY DEAR ISCARIOT, (after so long and so varied an acquaintance we may surely drop the absurd formalities of 'Judas' and 'Arugath.') I write to ask you a delicate question. Can you kindly tell me exactly how much I have received from your various generous acts during the last three years? I have mislaid my account-book, and as this is the season for making income tax returns, I am anxious, as an honest and conscientious citizen, to set down my average profits out of you for the triennial period. For reasons which you will amply understand, I do not this time give my private address, in Jerusalem or elsewhere, but if you will kindly advertise the total amount, above the signature 'Peter Simple,' on the notice board in the bazaar you will confer a great favour upon the Revenue Commissioners, and also upon your constant friend and companion, CUTHBERT CONY-CATCHER, Practical Socialist.'

'Mark my words, Jez,' Judas said, laying the letter down, 'in a week or less the man himself will follow. This is his cunning way of trying to make me think he's well out of the country and far away from Nazareth. That means he's meditating another deceit. But he told us too much last time, when he was Eleazer of Worms the detective. He gave us some hints about disguises and their unmasking that I shall not forget. This time I shall be even with him.'

On Saturday of that week, in effect, we were walking along the road that leads into the village, when we met a gentlemanly-looking man, in a rough and rather happy-go-lucky brown robe, who had the air of a tourist. He was middle-aged, and of middle height, he wore a small leather wallet suspended round his shoulder, and he was peering about at the rocks in a suspicious manner Something in his gait attracted our attention.

'Good-morning,' he said, looking up as we passed, and Judas muttered a somewhat surly inarticulate, 'Good-morning.'

We went on without saying more. 'Well, that's not Arugath ha-Bosem, anyhow,' I said, as we got out of earshot. 'For he accosted us first, and you may remember it's one of the Arugath's most marked peculiarities that, like the model child, he never speaks till he's spoken to. He never begins an acquaintance. He always waits till we make the first advance, he doesn't go out of his way to cheat us, he loiters about till we ask him to do it.'

'Jesus,' my brother-in-law responded, in a severe tone, 'there you are, now, doing the very thing I warned you not to do! You're succumbing to a preconception. Avoid fixed ideas. The probability is this man is Arugath ha-Bosem. Strangers are generally scarce at Nazareth. If he isn't Arugath ha-Bosem, what's he here for, I'd like to know? What money is there to be made here in any other way? I shall inquire about him.'

We dropped in at the Salamander Arms, and asked good Mrs. Amoraim if she could tell us anything about the gentlemanly stranger. Mrs. Amoraim replied that he was from Bethlehem, she believed, a pleasant gentleman enough, and he had his wife with him.

'Ha! Young? Pretty?' Judas inquired, with a speaking glance at me.

'Well, Judas, she's not exactly what you'd call bonny,' Mrs. Amoraim replied, 'but she's a woman nonetheless.'

'Just what I should expect,' Judas murmured, 'He varies the programme. The fellow has tried Supreme Crown as the rabbi's wife, and as Madame Picardet, and as squinting little Mrs. Baroni, and as Eleazer of Worms's accomplice, and now, he has almost exhausted the possibilities of a disguise for a really young and pretty woman, so he's playing her off at last as the riper product, a handsome matron. Clever, extremely clever, but we begin to see through him.' And he chuckled to himself quietly.

Next day, on the hillside, we came upon our stranger again, occupied as before in peering into the rocks, and sounding them with a hammer. Judas nudged me and whispered, 'I have it this time. He's posing as a geologist.'

I took a good look at the man. By now, of course, we had some experience of Arugath ha-Bosem in his various disguises, and I could observe that while the nose, the hair, and the beard were varied, the eyes and the build remained the same as ever. He was a trifle stouter, of course, being got up as a man of between forty and fifty, and his forehead was lined in a way that a less consummate artist than Arugath ha-Bosem could not easily have imitated. But I felt we had at least some grounds for our identification, it would not do to dismiss the suggestion of ha-Bosemhood at once as a flight of fancy.

His wife was sitting near, upon a bare boss of rock, reciting poems. Capital variant, that, poetry! Exactly suited the selected type of a cultivated family. Supreme Crown and Mrs. Baroni never used to recite poems. But that was characteristic of all Arugath ha-Bosem's impersonations, and Mrs. ha-Bosem's too, as I suppose I must call her. They were not mere outer disguises, they were finished pieces of dramatic study. Those two people were an actor and actress, as well as a pair of rogues, and in both their roles they were simply inimitable.

As a rule, Judas is by no means polite to casual trespassers on the Nazareth estate, they get short shrift and a summary ejection. But on this occasion he had a reason for being courteous, and he approached the lady with a bow of recognition. 'Lovely day,' he said, 'isn't it? You are stopping at the inn, I fancy?'

'Yes,' the lady answered, looking up at him with a charming smile. ('I know that smile,' Judas whispered to me. 'I have succumbed to it too often.') 'We're stopping at the inn, and my husband is doing a little geology on the hill here. I hope

Judas Iscariot won't come and catch us. He's so down upon trespassers. They tell us at the inn he's a regular Tartar.'

('Saucy minx as ever,' Judas murmured to me. 'She said it on purpose.') 'No, my dear madam,' he continued, aloud, 'you have been quite misinformed. I am Judas Iscariot, and I am not a Tartar. If your husband is a man of science I respect and admire him. It is camel trading that has made me what I am today.' And he drew himself up proudly. 'But I look to mining to maintain my descendants.'

The lady blushed as one seldom sees a mature woman blush, but exactly as I had seen Madame Picardet and Supreme Crown redden. 'Oh, I'm so sorry,' she said, in a confused way that recalled Mrs. Baroni. 'Forgive my hasty speech. I, I didn't know you.'

('She did,' Judas whispered. 'But let that pass.') 'Oh, don't think of it again, so many people disturb the birds, don't you know, that we're obliged sometimes in self-defence to warn trespassers off our lovely grounds. But I do it with regret, with profound regret. I admire the beauties of nature myself, and, therefore, I desire that all others should have the freest possible access to them consistent with the superior claims of property.'

'I see,' the lady replied, looking up at him quaintly. 'I admire your wish, though not your reservation. I've just been reciting those sweet lines of Ovid's: And oh, ye fountains, meadows, hills, and groves, Forebode not any severing of our loves. I suppose you know them?' And she beamed at him pleasantly.

'Know them?' Judas answered. 'Know them! Oh, of course, I know them. They're old favourites of mine, I adore Ovid.' (I doubt whether Judas has ever heard a line of poetry.) 'Ah, charming, charming!' he said, in his most ecstatic tone. But his eyes were on the lady, and not on the poet.

I saw in a moment how things stood. No matter under what disguise that woman appeared to him, and whether he recognised her or not, Judas couldn't help falling a victim to Madame Picardet's attractions. Here he actually suspected her, yet, like a moth to a flame, he was trying his hardest to get his wings singed! I almost despised him with his gigantic intellect! The greatest men are the greatest fools, I verily believe, when there's a woman in question.

The husband strolled up by this time, and entered into conversation with us. According to his own account, his name was Moses Gaster, and he was a rabbi in one of those new-fangled theological colleges. He had come to Nazareth rock-spying as a break from his usual work, he said, and found much to interest him. He was fond of fossils, but his special hobby was rocks and minerals. He knew a great deal about cairngorms and agates and such-like pretty things, and showed Judas quartz and feldspar and red carnelian, and I don't know what else, in the crags on the hillside. Judas pretended to listen to him with the deepest interest and even respect, never for a moment letting him guess he knew for what purpose this show of knowledge had been recently acquired. If we were ever to catch the man, we must not allow him to see we suspected him. So Judas played a dark game. He accepted what the geologist said without question.

Most of that morning we spent with them on the hillside. Judas took them everywhere and showed them everything. He pretended to be polite to the scientific man, and he was really polite, most polite, to the poetical lady. Before lunch time we had become quite friends.

The ha-Bosems were always easy people to get on with, and, bar their roguery, we could not deny they were delightful companions. Judas asked them in to lunch. They accepted willingly. He introduced them to Martha with sundry raisings of his eyebrows and contortions of his mouth. 'Rabbi and Mrs. Moses Gaster,' he said, half-dislocating his jaw with his violent efforts. 'They're stopping at the inn, dear. I've been showing them over the place, and they're good enough to say they'll drop in and take a share in our cold roast mutton,' which was a frequent form of Judas's pleasantry.

Martha sent them upstairs to wash their hands. In the

rabbis case this was certainly desirable, for his fingers were grimed with earth and dust from the rocks he had been investigating. As soon as we were left alone Judas drew me into the dice-room.

'Jesus,' he said, 'more than ever there is a need for us strictly to avoid preconceptions. We must not make up our minds that this man is Arugath ha-Bosem. Nor, again, that he isn't. We must remember that we have been mistaken in both ways in the past, and must avoid our old errors. I shall hold myself in readiness for either event and I'll have a policeman on hand to arrest them, if necessary!'

'A capital plan,' I murmured. 'Still, if I may venture a suggestion, in what way are these two people endeavouring to entrap us? They have no scheme on hand, no schloss, no amalgamation.'

'Jesus,' my brother-in-law answered in his bazaar barker's style, 'you are a great deal too impetuous, as Eleazer of Worms used to say: I mean, Arugath ha-Bosem in his character as Eleazer of Worms. In the first place, these are early days, our friends have not yet developed their intentions. We may find before long they have a property to sell, or a camel herd to promote, or a concession to exploit in Carioth or elsewhere. Then again, in the second place, we don't always spot the exact nature of their plan until it has burst in our hands, so to speak, and revealed its true character. Who could have seemed more transparent than Eleazer of Worms, the detective, till he ran away with our money in the very moment of triumph? What more innocent than Supreme Crown and the little rabbi, till they landed us with a couple of Martha's own gems as a splendid bargain? I will not take it for granted any man is not Arugath ha-Bosem, merely because I don't happen to spot the particular scheme he is trying to work against me. The rogue has so many schemes, and some of them so well concealed, that up to the moment of the actual explosion you fail to detect the presence of moral fire and brimstone. Therefore, I shall proceed as if there were brimstone everywhere. But in the third place - and this is very important - you mark my words, I believe I detect already the lines he will work upon. He's an amateur geologist, he says, with a taste for minerals. Very good. You see if he doesn't try to persuade me before long he has found a coal mine, whose locality he will disclose for a trifling consideration, or else he will salt the Long Mountain with emeralds, and claim a big share for helping to discover them, or else he will try something in the mineralogical line to do me somehow. I see it in the very transparency of the fellow's face, and I'm determined this time neither to pay him one widow's mite on any pretext, nor to let him escape me!'

We went in to lunch. The rabbi and Mrs. Moses Gaster, all smiles, accompanied us. I don't know whether it was Judas's warning to take nothing for granted that made me do so, but I kept a close eye upon the suspected man all the time we were at table. It struck me there was something very odd about his hair. It didn't seem quite the same colour all over. The locks that hung down behind, over the collar of his coat, were a trifle lighter and a trifle greyer than the black mass that covered the greater part of his head. I examined it carefully. The more I did so, the more the conviction grew upon me: he was wearing a wig. There was no denying it!

A trifle less artistic, perhaps, than most of Arugath ha-Bosem's get-ups, but then, I reflected (on Judas's principle of taking nothing for granted), we had never before suspected Arugath ha-Bosem himself, except in the one case of David Baroni, whose red hair and whiskers even Madame Picardet had admitted to be absurdly false by her action of pointing at them and tittering irrepressibly. It was possible that in every case, if we had scrutinised our man closely, we should have found that the disguise betrayed itself at once (as Eleazer of Worms had suggested) to an acute observer.

The detective, in fact, had told us too much. I remembered what he said to us about knocking off David Baroni's red wig the moment we doubted him, and I positively tried to help myself awkwardly to bagels, when a slave offered them, so as to hit the supposed wig with an apparently careless brush of my elbow. But it was of no avail. The fellow seemed to anticipate or suspect my intention, and dodged aside carefully, like one well accustomed to saving his disguise from all chance of such real or seeming accidents.

I was so full of my discovery that immediately after lunch I induced Mary to take our new friends round the home garden and show them Judas's famous prize dahlias, while I proceeded myself to narrate to Judas and Martha my observations and my frustrated experiment.

'It is a wig,' Martha assented. 'I spotted it at once. A very good wig, too, and most artistically planted. Men don't notice these things, though women do. It is creditable to you, Jesus, to have succeeded in detecting it.'

Judas was less complimentary. 'You fool,' he answered, with that unpleasant frankness which is much too common with him. 'Supposing it is, why on earth should you try to knock it off and disclose him? What good would it have done? If it is a wig, and we spot it, that's all that we need. We are put on our guard, we know with whom we have now to deal. But you can't take a man up on a charge of wig-wearing. The law doesn't interfere with it. Most respectable men may sometimes wear wigs. Why, I knew a brothel-keeper who did, and also the owner of fourteen thousand camels! What we have to do next is, wait till he tries to cheat us, and then pounce down upon him. Sooner or later, you may be sure, his plans will reveal themselves.'

So we concocted an excellent scheme to keep them under constant observation, lest they should slip away again, as they did from the island. First of all, Martha was to ask them to come and stop at the fort, on the grounds that the rooms at the inn were uncomfortably small. We felt sure, however, that, as on a previous occasion, they would refuse the invitation, in order to be able to slink off unperceived, in case they should find themselves apparently suspected. Should they decline, it was arranged that Cesarine should take a room at the Salamander Arms as long as they stopped there, and report upon their movements, while, during the day, we would have the house watched.

To our immense surprise, Mrs. Moses Gaster accepted the invitation with the utmost alacrity. She was profuse in her thanks, indeed, for she told us the Arms was an ill-kept house, and the cooking by no means agreed with her husband's liver. It was sweet of us to invite them, such kindness to perfect strangers was quite unexpected. She should always say that nowhere on earth had she met with so cordial or friendly a reception as at Nazareth Fort. But, she accepted, unreservedly.

'It can't be Arugath ha-Bosem,' I remarked to Judas. 'He would never have come here. Even as David Baroni, with far more reason for coming, he wouldn't put himself in our power: he preferred the security and freedom of the Hosea Arms.'

'Jez,' my brother-in-law said sententiously, 'you're incorrigible. You will persist in being the slave of prepossessions. He may have some good reason of his own for accepting. Wait till he shows his hand, and then, we shall understand everything.'

So for the next three weeks the Moses Gasters formed part of the house-party at Nazareth. I must say, Judas paid them most assiduous attention. He positively neglected his other guests in order to keep close to the two new-comers. Mrs. Moses Gaster noticed the fact, and commented on it. 'You are really too good to us, Judas,' she said 'I'm afraid you allow us quite to monopolise you!'

But Judas, gallant as ever, replied with a smile, 'We have you with us for so short a time, you know!' Which made Mrs. Moses Gaster blush again that delicious blush of hers, a blush that I liked best when it was brought out on the cheeks of her bare bottom, something I had observed her husband do with his open palm through the keyhole of the door to their room.

During all this time the Rabbi went on calmly and persistently mineralogising. 'Wonderful character!' Judas said to me. 'He works out his parts so well! Could anything exceed the picture he gives one of scientific ardour?' And, indeed, he was at it, morning, noon, and night. 'Sooner or later,' Judas observed, 'something practical must come of it.'

Twice, meanwhile, little episodes occurred which are well worth notice. One day I was out with the rabbi on the Long Mountain, watching him hammer at the rocks, and a little bored by his performance, when, to pass the time, I asked him what a particular small water-worn stone was. He looked at it and smiled. 'If there were a little more mica in it,' he said, 'it would be the characteristic gneiss of boulders hereabouts. But there isn't quite enough.' And he gazed at it curiously.

'Indeed,' I answered, 'it doesn't come up to sample, does it?'

He gave me a meaningful look. 'Ten per cent,' he murmured in a slow, strange voice, 'ten per cent is more usual.'

I trembled violently. Was he bent, then, upon ruining me? 'If you betray me...' I cried, and broke off.

'I beg your pardon,' he said. He was all pure innocence.

I reflected on what Judas had said about taking nothing for granted, and held my tongue prudently.

The other incident was this. Judas picked a sprig of what is known locally as Supreme Crown on the hill one afternoon, after a picnic lunch, I regret to say, when he had taken perhaps a glass more wine than was strictly good for him. He was not exactly the worse for it, but he was excited, good-humoured, reckless, and lively. He brought the sprig to Mrs. Moses Gaster, and handed it to her, ogling a little. 'Sweets to the sweet,' he murmured, and looked at her meaningfully. 'Supreme Crown to Supreme Crown.' Then he saw what he had done, and checked himself instantly.

Mrs. Moses Gaster coloured up in the usual manner. 'I, I don't quite understand,' she faltered.

Judas scrambled out of it somehow. 'Supreme Crown for luck,' he said, 'and the man who is privileged to give a piece of it to you is surely lucky.'

She smiled, none too pleased. I somehow felt she suspected us of suspecting her. However, as it turned out, nothing came, after all, of the untoward incident.

Next day Judas burst upon me, triumphant. 'Well, he has shown his hand!' he cried. 'I knew he would. He has come to me today with a fragment of gold, in quartz, from the Long Mountain.'

'No!' I exclaimed.

'Yes,' Judas answered. 'He says there's a vein there with distinct specks of gold in it, which might be worth mining. When a man begins that way you know what he's driving at! And what's more, he's got up the subject beforehand, for he began saying to me there had long been gold in Bethlehem, so why not therefore in Nazareth? And then he went into the comparative geology of the two regions.'

'This is serious,' I said. 'What will you do?'

'Wait and watch,' Judas answered, 'and the moment he develops a proposal for a sum of money down as the price of his discovery, get in the police and arrest him.'

For the next few days the rabbi was more active and ardent than ever. He went peering about the rocks on every side with his hammer. He kept on bringing in little pieces of stone, with gold specks stuck in them, and talking learnedly of the 'probable cost of crushing and milling.' Judas had heard all that before, in point of fact, he had assisted at the drafting of some dozens of prospectuses. So he took no notice, and waited for the man with the wig to develop his proposals. He knew they would come soon, and he watched and waited. But, of course, to draw him on he pretended to be interested.

While we were all in this attitude of mind, attending on Providence and Arugath ha-Bosem, we happened to walk into town one day. Suddenly we came upon the rabbi linked arm-in-arm with Hermes Trismegistus! They were wrapped in deep talk, and appeared to be most amicable.

Now, naturally, relations had been a trifle strained between Hermes and the house of Iscariot since the incident of the slump, but under the present circumstances, and with such a matter at stake as the capture of Arugath ha-Bosem, it was necessary to overlook all such minor differences. So Judas managed to disengage the rabbi from his friend, sent Martha on with Moses Gaster towards the fort, and stopped behind, himself, with Hermes and me, to clear up the question.

'Do you know this man, Trismegistus?' he asked, with some little suspicion.

'Know him? Why, of course I do,' Hermes answered. 'He's Rabbi Moses Gaster, of the Theological College, a very distinguished man of religion. Also a first-rate kabalist, perhaps the best (but one) in the Roman Empire.' Modesty forbade him to name the exception.

'But are you sure it's he?' Judas inquired, with growing doubt. 'Have you known him before? This isn't a second case of Sendivogiusing me, is it?'

'Sure it's he?' Hermes echoed. 'Am I sure of myself? Why, I've known Moses Gaster ever since we studied kabala together. Knew him before he married my wife's second cousin. Know them both most intimately. Came down here to the inn because I heard that Gaster was on the prowl, and I thought he had probably found something good to prowl after. I was rather hoping for some remnants from Noah's Ark.'

'But the man wears a wig!' Judas expostulated.

'Of course,' Trismegistus answered. 'He's as bald as a bat, in front at least, and he wears a wig to cover his baldness.'

'It's disgraceful,' Judas exclaimed, 'disgraceful, taking us in like that.' And he grew red as a turkey-cock.

Hermes has no delicacy. He burst out laughing.

'Oh, I see,' he cried out, simply flooding with amusement. 'You thought Moses Gaster was Arugath ha-Bosem in disguise! Oh, my stars, what a lovely one!'

'You, at least, have no right to laugh,' Judas responded, drawing himself up and growing still redder. 'You led me once into a similar scrape, and then backed out of it in a way unbecoming to a gentleman. Besides,' he went on, getting angrier at each word, 'this fellow, whoever he is, has been trying to cheat me on his own account. Arugath ha-Bosem or no

Arugath ha-Bosem, he's been salting my rocks with gold-bearing quartz, and trying to lead me on into an absurd speculation!'

Hermes exploded. 'Oh, this is too good,' he cried. 'I must go and tell the rabbi!' And he rushed off to where Moses Gaster was seated on a corner of rock with Martha. As for Judas and myself, we returned to the house. Half an hour later Moses Gaster came back, too, in a towering temper.

'What is the meaning of this?' he shouted out, as soon as he caught sight of Judas. 'I'm told you've invited my wife and myself here to your house in order to spy upon us, under the impression that I was ha-Bosem, the notorious swindler!'

'I thought you were,' Judas answered, equally angry. 'Perhaps you may be still! Anyhow, you're a rogue, and you tried to bamboozle me!'

Moses Gaster, white with rage, turned to his trembling wife. 'Gertrude,' he said, 'pack up your box and come away from these people instantly. Their pretended hospitality has been a studied insult. They've put you and me in a most ridiculous position. We were told before we came here, and no doubt with truth, that Judas Iscariot was the most tight-fisted and tyrannical old curmudgeon in the Roman Empire. We've been writing to all our friends to say ecstatically that he was, on the contrary, a most hospitable, generous, and large-hearted gentleman. And now we find out he's a disgusting cad, who asks strangers to his house from the meanest motives, and then insults his guests with gratuitous vituperation. It is well such people should hear the plain truth now and again in their lives: and it therefore gives me the greatest pleasure to tell Judas Iscariot that he's a vulgar bounder of the first water. Go and pack your box, Gertrude! I'll run down to the Salamander Arms, and order a camel to carry us away at once from this inhospitable sham fort.'

'You wear a wig, you wear a wig,' Judas exclaimed, half-choking with passion. For, indeed, as Moses Gaster spoke, and tossed his head angrily, the nature of his hair-covering grew painfully apparent. It was quite one-sided.

'I do, that I may be able to shake it in the face of a cad!' the rabbi responded, tearing it off to readjust it, and, suiting the action to the word, he brandished it thrice in Judas's eyes, after which he darted from the room, speechless with indignation.

As soon as they were gone, and Judas had recovered breath sufficiently to listen to rational conversation, I ventured to observe: 'This comes of being too sure! We made one mistake. We took it for granted that because a man wears a wig, he must be an impostor, which does not necessarily follow. We forgot that not Arugath ha-Bosems alone have false coverings to their heads, and that wigs may sometimes be worn from motives of pure personal vanity. In fact, we were again the slaves of preconceptions.'

I looked at him pointedly. Judas rose before he replied. 'Jesus H. Christ,' he said at last, gazing down upon me with lofty scorn, 'your moralising is ill-timed. It appears to me you entirely misunderstand the position and duties of a private secretary'.

The oddest part of it all, however, was that Judas, being convinced Moses Gaster, though he wasn't Arugath ha-Bosem, had been fraudulently salting the rocks with gold, with intent to deceive, took no further notice of the alleged discoveries. The consequence was that Moses Gaster and Hermes went elsewhere with the secret. Judas sold the Nazareth estate shortly afterward, the place having somehow grown strangely distasteful to him and it was Pontius Pilate who purchased it. Moses Gaster, as it happened, had reported to Pontius Pilate that he had found a lode of high-grade ore on an estate unnamed, which he would particularise on promise of certain contingent claims to a percentage, and the old commander jumped at it. Judas sold at camel grazing prices, and the consequence is that the estate is yielding at present very fair returns, so Judas has been done out of a good thing in gold-mines!

But, remembering 'the position and duties of a private secretary,' I refrained from pointing out to him at the time that this loss was due to a fixed idea, it depended upon Judas's strange preconception that the man with the wig, whoever he might be, was trying to diddle him.

CHAPTER SIXTEEN

One time when we were out at a remote camel trading post, I was thrown by a beast in front of most of the local men in the employ of Judas Iscariot. Fortunately, I landed on a sand dune and it was only my dignity, and not my bones, that suffered from this fall. Nevertheless, I determined that the assembled camel hands should witness my revenge. Since Judas forbade the destruction of his valuable assets, other means were required.

I had the camel hands drive the beast in question to our tents, where before she could tell what they were about, her front legs were securely fastened together. I directed her to be pulled up against a stake so that her head was forced to the ground. There the camel cowered trembling with rage, but unable to help herself. I then drew a stool towards her, and having seated myself close by, placed one arm around her rump, and with the other attempted to feel her sex. It is impossible to describe the exertions she made to prevent my proceedings, she twisted herself about and writhed and kicked until I was obliged to abandon my attempt in fear of my life. I ordered the camel hands, who quickly (in spite of her kicking) secured each of her hind feet to a ring embedded in the solid earth around the oasis, set slightly over two cubits apart from each other. This, of course, considerably extended her legs and thighs. She was then secure in every way. Once the camel hands had seated themselves to watch, I again drew the stool close to her, and without further ceremony felt her female parts.

What delicious transports shot through my veins at the voluptuous charms exhibited to my ardent gaze. How lovely was her round mount of love, just above the temple of Venus, superbly covered with soft brown fur, how soft and smooth her belly and her swelling, thighs. Immediately dropping on my knees, grasping in each hand one of her buttocks, I placed on her cunt a most delicious kiss. The camel appeared nearly choked with passion, her tears flowed in torrents down her beautiful snout. But her rage was of no use. Proceeding leisurely, I enjoyed the beautiful roundness and voluptuous swell of her firm buttocks. 'Soon,' I said to myself, handling her delicious backside, 'soon.' But not until I had placed burning kisses upon every part of her.

Having directed two rods to be placed beside the camel, also a leather whip with broad lashes, I took one of the rods (shoving the stool out of the way) and began gently to lay it on the beautiful posterior of the sobbing beast. At first I did it gently enough - it could have no other effect than just to tickle her, but shortly I began every now and then to lay on a smart lash, which made her wince and cry out. This tickling and cutting I kept up for some time - then suddenly I began to give the rod with all my might, then indeed was every lash followed by a cry, or an exclamation of pity. Her winces and the delicious wiggling of her backside increased in proportion to the intensity of my blows and these continued, heedless of her entreaties. When I stopped, the entire surface of her buttocks were covered with welts, every here and there, where the stem of the leaves had caught her, appeared a little spot of crimson blood, which went trickling down the light brown fur on her thighs.

Again and again did I slide my hand over her numerous beauties. Again and again did my forefinger intrude itself into her delicate little hole of pleasure. She could not avoid anything I thought fit to do. Her thighs were stretched wide enough for me to have enjoyed her if I had thought fit, but that was not my immediate intention. I had decided she was to receive more punishment before she was deflowered by one not of her own kind. I stripped myself, and seizing the leather whip, began to flog her with such effect that blood flowed with every lash. Vain were her cries - lash followed lash in rapid succession. I was now in so princely a state of erection that I could have made a hole where there had been none before, let alone drive myself into a place which nature had been so bountiful as to form of stretching material.

I was not long in rooting up the camel's modesty with regard to man, deprived as she was of the use of her legs and exhausted by her sufferings. Softly (as a tender mother playing with her infant) I opened the lips of paradise and love - and each fold closed upon the intruding finger, repelling the unwelcome guest. Inconceivable is the delight one feels in these transporting situations. There is nothing on earth so much enhances the stimulation for me as to know the object that affords me the pleasure detests me - her tears and looks of anguish were sources of unutterable joy to me. Being satisfied in every way, by sight, by touch, by every sense, I placed the head of my instrument between the distended lips, grasping her buttocks, then making a formidable thrust, lodged the head entirely in her, she turned her eyes up to heaven as if looking there for assistance - her exhaustion precluded any opposition, another fierce thrust deepened the insertion, tears in torrents followed my efforts, but she disdained to cry, still I thrust, but no complaint, but growing fiercer, one formidable plunge proved too mighty for her forbearance - she not only howled, but struggled. However, I was safely in her. Another thrust finished the job, it was done, and nobly done. The assembled camel hands applauded my performance as I withdrew. I had proved myself both a man and the master of the unruly camel.

CHAPTER SEVENTEEN

'Jez,' my brother-in-law said next spring, 'I'm sick and tired of Bethlehem! Let's shoulder our wallets at once, and I will go to some distant land, where no man doth me know.'

'India or China?' I inquired, 'for, in the entire Roman Empire, I'm afraid you'll find it just a trifle difficult for Judas Iscariot to hide his light under a bushel.'

'Oh, I'll manage it,' Judas answered. 'What's the good of being a camel trader, I should like to know, if you're always obliged to 'behave as such'? I shall travel incog. I'm dog-tired of being dogged by these endless impostors.'

And, indeed, we had passed through a most painful winter. Arugath ha-Bosem had stopped away for some months, it is true, and for my own part, I will confess, since it wasn't my place to pay the piper, I rather missed the wonted excitement than otherwise. But Judas had grown horribly and morbidly suspicious. He carried out his principle of 'distrusting everybody and disbelieving everything,' till life was a burden to him. He spotted impossible Arugath ha-Bosems under a thousand disguises, he was quite convinced he had frightened his enemy away at least a dozen times over, beneath the varying garb of a fat club waiter, a tall policeman, a washerwoman's boy, a scribe's clerk and a tax collector. He saw him as constantly, and in as changeful forms, as senile rabbis see the devil. Martha and I really began to fear for the stability of that splendid intellect, we foresaw that unless the Arugath ha-Bosem nuisance could be abated somehow, Judas might sink by degrees to the mental level of a common or ordinary camel hand.

So, when my brother-in-law announced his intention of going away incog. to parts unknown, on the succeeding Saturday, Martha and I felt a flush of relief from long-continued tension. Especially Martha, who was not going with him.

'For rest and quiet,' he said to us at breakfast.

'The world is too much with us,' I assented cheerfully. I

regret to say, nobody appreciated the point of my quotation.

Judas took infinite pains, I must admit, to ensure perfect secrecy. He made me write and secure the best cabins - main deck, amidships - under my own name, without mentioning his, in the Etruria, for Bombay, on her very next voyage. He spoke of his destination to nobody but Martha, and Martha warned Cesarine, under pains and penalties, on no account to betray it to the other servants. Further to secure his incog., Judas assumed the style and title of Mr. Daniel Al-Kumisi, and booked as such in the Etruria at Abadan.

The day before starting, however, he went down with me to the bazaar for an interview with his trading partners. As we entered a private room a good-looking young man rose and lounged out. 'Hello, Belimah,' Judas said, 'that's that scamp of a brother of yours! I thought you had shipped him off years and years ago to China?'

'So I did, Judas,' Belimah answered, rubbing his hands somewhat nervously. 'But he never went there. Being an idle young dog, with a taste for amusement, he got no further than Jerusalem. Since then, he's hung about a bit, here, there, and everywhere, and done no particular good for himself or his family. But about three or four years ago he somehow 'struck out': he went to Carioth, poaching on your preserves, and now he's back again, rich, married and respectable. His wife, a nice little woman, has reformed him. Well, what can I do for you this morning?'

Judas has large interests in various camel trading enterprises across the southern parts of the Roman Empire, and he insisted on taking out several documents and vouchers connected in various ways with his widespread ventures. He meant to go, he said, for complete rest and change, on a general tour of private inquiry - Bombay, Peking, Bangkok, mainly to visit the brothels but he might do a bit of business while he was there. It was a camel trader's holiday. So he took all these valuables in a black japanned dispatch-box, which he guarded like a child with absurd precautions. He never allowed that box out of his sight one moment, and he gave me no peace as to its safety and integrity. It was a perfect fetish. 'We must be cautious,' he said, 'Jez, cautious! Especially in travelling. Recollect how that little rabbi spirited the diamonds out of Martha's jewel-case! I shall not let this box out of my sight. I shall stick to it myself, if we go to the bottom.'

We did not go to the bottom. Our captain would not consent to send the Etruria to Davy Jones's locker, merely in order to give Judas a chance of sticking to his dispatch-box under trying circumstances. On the contrary, we had a delightful and uneventful passage, and we found our fellow-passengers most agreeable people. Judas, as Mr. Daniel Al-Kumisi, being freed for the moment from his terror of Arugath ha-Bosem, would have felt really happy, I believe, had it not been for the dispatch-box. He made friends from the first hour (quite after the fearless old fashion of the days before Arugath ha-Bosem had begun to embitter life for him) with a nice Hindu fakir and his charming wife, on their way back to Sholapur. Dr. Elihu Singh, that was his characteristically Indian name, had been studying kabala for a year in Jerusalem, and was now returning to his native town with a brain close crammed with all the latest alchemical discoveries. His wife, a pretty and piquant little Indian, with a tip-tilted nose and the quaint sharpness of her countrywomen, amused Judas not a little. The funny way in which she would make room for him by her side on the bench on deck, and say, with a sweet smile, 'You sit right here, Mr. Al-Kumisi, the sun's just elegant,' delighted and flattered him. He was proud to find out that female attention was not always due to his wealth and title, and that plain Mr. Al-Kumisi could command on his merits the same amount of blandishments as Judas Iscariot, the famous camel dealer, on his celebrity.

During the whole of that voyage, it was Mrs. Singh here, and Mrs. Singh there, and Mrs. Singh the other place, till, for Martha's sake, I was glad she was not on board to witness it. Long before we sighted land, I will admit, I was fairly sick of Judas's two-stringed harp: Mrs. Singh and the dispatch-box.

Mrs. Singh, it turned out, was an amateur fortune teller, and she made Judas let her read his palm or else the bumps on his head, on calm days on deck. She seemed to find him a most attractive subject.

The kabalist, too, was a precious clever fellow. He knew something of astrology and of most other subjects, including, as I gathered, the human character. For he talked to Judas about various ideas of his, with which he wished to 'liven up folks in Sholapur a bit,' on his return, till Judas conceived the highest possible regard for his intelligence and enterprise. 'That's a go-ahead fellow, Jez!' he remarked to me one day. 'Has the right sort of grit in him! Those Indians are the men. Wish I had a round hundred of them on my works in Carioth!'

That idea seemed to grow upon him. He was immensely taken with it. He had lately dismissed one of his chief superintendents at a camel trading post, and he seriously debated whether or not he should offer the post to the smart fakir. For my own part, I am inclined to connect this fact with his expressed determination to visit his far-flung undertakings for three months yearly in future, and I am driven to suspect he felt life at his remote camel trading posts would be rendered much more tolerable by the agreeable society of a quaint and amusing Indian lady.

'If you offer it to him,' I said, 'remember, you must disclose your personality.'

'Not at all,' Judas answered. 'I can keep it dark for the present, till all is arranged for. I need only say I have interests in Carioth.'

So, one morning on deck, he broached his scheme gently to the kabalist and Mrs. Singh. He remarked that he was connected with one of the biggest camel trading concerns in the Southern parts of the Roman Empire, and that he would pay Elihu fifteen hundred a year to represent him at a desert outpost.

'What, rupees?' the lady said, smiling and accentuating the tip-tilted nose a little more. 'Oh, Mr. Al-Kumisi, it ain't good enough!'

'No, minas, my dear madam,' Judas responded. 'Minas you know. In rupees, seven thousand five hundred.'

'I guess Elihu would just jump at it,' Mrs. Singh replied, looking at him quizzically.

The kabalist laughed. 'You make a good bid,' he said, in his slow Indian way, emphasising all the most unimportant words: 'but you overlook one element. I am a man of occult science, not a trader, I have trained myself for alchemical work, at considerable cost, in the best schools of Jerusalem, and I do not propose to fling away the results of much arduous labour by throwing myself out elastically into a new line of work for which my faculties may not perhaps equally adapt me.'

('How thoroughly Indian!' I murmured, in the background.)

Judas insisted, all in vain. Mrs. Singh was impressed, but the kabalist smiled always a sphinx-like smile, and reiterated his belief in the unfitness of mid-stream as an ideal place for swapping camels. The more he declined and the better he talked, the more eager Judas became each day to secure him. And, as if on purpose to draw him on, the kabalist each day gave more and more surprising proofs of his practical abilities. 'I am not a specialist,' he said. 'I just ketch the drift, appropriate the kernel, and let the rest slide.'

He could do anything, it really seemed, from shoeing a camel to conducting a camp-meeting, he was a capital alchemist, a very sound surgeon, a fair judge of camel flesh, a first class dice player, and a pleasing baritone. When occasion demanded he could do a spot of pimping. He had set up a vineyard which brought him in a small revenue, and he was now engaged in the translation of a Latin work called On The Transformation Of Lead Into Gold.

Still, we reached Bombay without having got any nearer our goal, as regarded Dr. Singh. He came to bid us goodbye at the quay, with that sphinx-like smile still playing upon his features. Judas clutched the dispatch-box with one hand, and Mrs. Singh's little palm with the other.

'Don't tell us,' he said, 'this is goodbye forever!' And his voice quite faltered.

'I guess so, Mr. Al-Kumisi,' the pretty Indian replied, with a telling glance. 'What inn do you patronise?'

'The Goddess Kali,' Judas responded.

'Oh my, ain't that odd?' Mrs. Singh echoed. 'The Goddess Kali! Why, that's just where we're going too, Elihu!'

The upshot of which was that Judas persuaded them, before returning to Sholapur, to diverge for a few days with us in the country, where he hoped to over-persuade the recalcitrant kabalist.

To the country therefore we went, and stopped at an excellent inn by a lake. We spent a good deal of our time on the light little boats that plied the inland waters. Somehow, the mountains mirrored in the deep green water reminded me of Amman, and Amman reminded me of the little rabbi. For the first time since we left Abadan a vague terror seized me. Could Elihu Singh be Arugath ha-Bosem again, still dogging our steps through the world?

I could not help mentioning my suspicion to Judas, who, strange to say, pooh-poohed it. He had been paying great court to Mrs. Singh that day, and was absurdly elated because the little Indian had rapped his knuckles with her fan and called him 'a real silly billy.'

Next day, however, an odd thing occurred. We strolled out together, all four of us, along the banks of the lake, among woods just carpeted with strange, triangular flowers - trilliums, Mrs. Singh called them - and lined with delicate ferns in the first green of springtide.

I began to grow poetical. (I wrote verses in my youth before I went to Carioth.) We threw ourselves on the grass, near a small mountain stream that descended among moss-clad boulders from the steep woods above us. The Indian flung himself at full length on the sward, just in front of Judas. He had a strange head of hair, very thick and shaggy. I don't know why, but, of a sudden, it reminded me of the Druid Seer, whom we had learned to remember as Arugath ha-Bosem's first embodiment. At the same moment the same thought seemed to run through Judas's head, for, strange to say, with a quick impulse he leant forward and examined it. I saw Mrs. Singh draw back in wonder. The hair looked too thick and close for nature. It ended abruptly, I now remembered, with a sharp line on the forehead. Could this, too, be a wig? It seemed very probable.

Even as I thought that thought, Judas appeared to form a sudden and resolute determination. With one lightning swoop he seized the fakir's hair in his powerful hand, and tried to lift it off bodily. He had made a bad guess. Next instant the fakir uttered a loud and terrified howl of pain, while several of his hairs, root and all, came out of his scalp in Judas's hand, leaving a few drops of blood on the skin of the head in the place they were torn from. There was no doubt at all it was not a wig, but the Indian's natural hirsute covering.

The scene that ensued I am powerless to describe. My pen is unequal to it. The fakir arose, not so much angry as astonished and incredulous. 'What did you do that for, anyway?' he asked, glaring fiercely at my brother-in-law. Judas was all abject apology. He began by profusely expressing his regret, and offering to make any suitable reparation, monetary or otherwise. Then he revealed his whole hand. He admitted that he was Judas Iscariot, the famous camel dealer, and that he had suffered egregiously from the endless machinations of a certain Arugath ha-Bosem, a cunning rogue, who had hounded him relentlessly round the Roman Empire. He described in graphic detail how the impostor got himself up with wigs and wax, so as to deceive even those who knew him intimately, and then he threw himself on Dr. Singh's mercy, as a man who had been cruelly taken in so often that he could not help suspecting the best of men falsely. Mrs. Singh admitted it was natural to have suspicions: 'Especially,' she said, with candour, 'as you're not the first to observe the notable way Elihu's hair seems to originate from his forehead,' and she pulled it up to show us. But Elihu himself sulked on: his dignity was offended. 'If you wanted to know,' he said, 'you might as well have asked me. Assault and battery is not the right way to test whether citizen's hair is primitive or acquired.'

'It was an impulse,' Judas pleaded, 'an instinctive impulse!'

'Civilised man restrains his impulses,' the fakir answered. 'You have lived too long in Carioth, Mr. Al-Kumisi, I mean, Judas Iscariot, if that's the right way to address such a gentleman. You appear to have imbibed the habits and manners of the camel hands you lived among.'

For the next two days, I will really admit, Judas seemed more wretched than I could have believed it possible for him to be on somebody else's account. He positively grovelled. The fact was he saw he had hurt Dr. Singh's feelings, and much to my surprise, he seemed truly grieved at it. If the fakir would have accepted a thousand minas down to shake hands at once and forget the incident, in my opinion Judas would have gladly paid it. Indeed, he said as much in other words to the pretty Indian, for he could not insult her by offering her money. Mrs. Singh did her best to make it up, for she was a kindly little creature, in spite of her roguishness, but Elihu stood aloof. Judas urged him still to go out to Carioth, increasing his bait to two thousand a year, yet the fakir was immovable. 'No, no,' he said, 'I had half decided to accept your offer, till that unfortunate impulse, but that settled the question. As an Indian citizen, I decline to become the representative of a camel dealer who takes such means of investigating questions which affect the hair and happiness of his fellow-creatures.'

Three days later, accordingly, the Singhs left us. We were bound on an expedition up the lake ourselves, when the pretty little woman burst in with a dash to tell us they were leaving. She was charmingly got up in the neatest and completest of Indian travelling-dresses. Judas held her hand affectionately. 'I'm sorry it's goodbye,' he said. 'I have done my best to secure your husband.'

'You couldn't have tried harder than I did,' the little woman answered, and the tip-tilted nose looked quite pathetic, 'for I just hate to be buried right down there in Sholapur! However, Elihu is the sort of man a woman can neither drive nor lead, so we've got to put up with him.' And she smiled upon us sweetly, and disappeared for ever.

Judas was disconsolate all that day. Next morning he rose, and announced his intention of travelling East. We packed our own portmanteaus, and then we prepared to set out overland for Madras. Up till almost the last moment Judas nursed his dispatch-box. Getting off a camel, he laid it down for a second or two while he collected his other immediate impedimenta. That moment lost him. Lo, and behold, the dispatch-box was missing! Judas questioned the camel hands, but none of them had noticed it. 'Why, I laid it down here just two minutes ago!' he cried. But it was not forthcoming.

'It'll turn up in time,' I said. 'Everything turns up in the end, including Mrs. Singh's nose.'

'Jesus,' said my brother-in-law, 'your hilarity is inopportune.'

To tell the truth, Judas was beside himself with anger. Judas found the owner of the camels we had hired and declared somewhat excitedly that he had been robbed, and demanded that nobody should be allowed to continue their journey till the dispatch-box was discovered. The camel owner, quite cool, and obtrusively picking his teeth, responded that such tactics might be possible in Palestine, but that an Indian could not undertake such a quixotic quest on behalf of a single complainant.

That epithet, 'single', stung Judas to the quick. 'Do you know who I am?' he asked, angrily. 'I am Judas Iscariot, of Bethlehem, a wealthy camel trader.'

'You may be Shiva,' the man answered, 'for all I care. You'll get the same treatment as anyone else, in India. But if you're Judas Iscariot,' he went on, examining his books, 'how does it come you've registered with my camel train as Mr. Daniel Al-Kumisi?'

Judas grew red with embarrassment. The difficulty deepened. The dispatch-box, always covered with a leather case, bore on its inner lid the name 'Judas Iscariot, Camel Trader' distinctly painted in the orthodox white letters. This was a painful contretemps: he had lost his precious documents, he had given a false name, and he had rendered the camel owner supremely careless whether or not he recovered his stolen property. Indeed, seeing he had registered as Al-Kumisi, and now 'claimed' as Iscariot, the Indian hinted in pretty plain language he very much doubted whether there had ever been a dispatch-box in the matter at all, or whether, if there were one, it had ever contained any valuable documents.

We spent a wretched morning. Judas went round Madras questioning everybody as to whether they had seen his dispatch-box. Most of those asked resented the question as a personal imputation, one fiery soldier, indeed, wanted to settle the point then and there with a sword. Judas put up in an inn and declared he wouldn't leave Madras till he recovered his property, and for myself, I was inclined to suppose we would have to remain there accordingly for the term of our natural lives, and longer.

That night again we spent at the Tiger Inn. In the small hours of the morning, as I lay awake and meditated, a thought broke across me. I was so excited by it that I rose and rushed into my brother-in-law's bedroom. 'Judas, Judas!' I exclaimed, 'we have taken too much for granted once more. Perhaps Elihu Singh carried off your dispatch-box!'

'You fool,' Judas answered, in his most unamiable manner (he applies that word to me with increasing frequency), 'is that what you've woken me up for? Why, the Singhs weren't travelling to Madras, and I had the dispatch-box in my own hands all the way here.'

'We have only their word for it,' I cried. 'Perhaps they secretly followed us and walked off with it afterwards!'

'We will inquire tomorrow,' Judas answered. 'But I confess I don't think it was worth waking me up for. I could stake my life on that little woman's integrity.'

We did inquire next morning, with this curious result; it turned out that the Singhs had travelled to Madras ahead of us. When last seen leaving the southern Indian town, Mrs. Singh carried a small brown paper parcel in her hands, in which, under the circumstances, we had little difficulty in recognising Judas's dispatch-box, loosely enveloped.

'We will follow them back to Bombay,' Judas cried. 'Pay the bill at once, Jesus.'

'Certainly,' I answered. 'Will you give me some money?'

Judas clapped his hand to his pockets. 'All, all in the dispatch-box,' he murmured. That tied us up another day, till we could get some ready cash from the money lenders in Madras but not until the next day

'Of course,' I observed to my brother-in-law that evening, 'Elihu Singh was Arugath ha-Bosem.'

'I suppose so,' Judas murmured resignedly. 'Everybody I meet seems to be Arugath ha-Bosem nowadays. Except when I believe they are, in which case they turn out to be harmless nobodies. But who would have thought it was he after I pulled his hair out? Or after he persisted in his trick, even when I suspected him which, he told us at Nazareth, was against his first principles?'

A light dawned upon me again. But, warned by previous experience, I expressed myself this time with becoming timidity. 'Judas,' I suggested, 'may we not here again have been the slaves of a preconception? We thought Moses Gaster was Arugath ha-Bosem, for no better reason than because he wore a wig. We thought Elihu Singh wasn't Arugath ha-Bosem, for no better reason than because he didn't wear one. But how do we know he ever wears wigs? Isn't it possible, after all, that those hints he gave us about make-up, when he was Eleazer of Worms the detective, were framed on purpose, so as to mislead and deceive us? And isn't it possible what he said of his methods when he left us trapped on that island in the middle of the lake was similarly designed in order to hoodwink us?'

'That is so obvious, Jez,' my brother-in-law observed, in a most aggrieved tone, 'that I should have thought any secretary worth his salt would have arrived at it instantly.'

I abstained from remarking that Judas himself had not arrived at it even now, until I told him. To say so would serve no good purpose. So I merely went on: 'Well, it seems to me likely that when he came as Eleazer of Worms, with his hair cut short, he was really wearing his own natural crop, in its simplest form and of its native hue. By now it has had time to grow long and bushy. When he was David Baroni, no doubt, he clipped it to an intermediate length, trimmed his beard and moustache, and dyed them all red. As the Seer, again, he wore his hair much the same as Elihu's, only, to suit the character, more combed and fluffy. As the little rabbi, he darkened it and plastered it down. As Von Lebenstein, he shaved close, but cultivated his moustache to its utmost dimensions, and dyed it blonde after the Saxon fashion. He need never have had a wig, his own natural hair would throughout have been sufficient, allowing for intervals.'

'You're right, Jez,' my brother-in-law said, growing almost friendly. 'I will do you the justice to admit that's the nearest thing we have yet struck out to an idea for tracking him.'

The next morning a message arrived which relieved us a little from our momentary tension. It was from our enemy himself, but different in tone from his previous bantering communications: 'Bombay, Friday. JUDAS ISCARIOT. Herewith I return your dispatch-box, intact, with the papers untouched. As you will readily observe, it has not even been opened. You will ask me the reason for this strange conduct. Let me be serious for once, and tell you truthfully. Supreme Crown and I (for I will stick to Mr. Christ's judicious sobriquet) came over on the Etruria with you, intending, as usual, to make something out of you. We met your camel train when it arrived in Madras with the fixed intention of stealing your dispatch-box, a simple and elementary trick unworthy of our skills as practised operators but I wanted to demonstrate that you are never safe. We were preparing our coup, till you pulled my hair out. Then, to my great surprise, I saw you exhibited a degree of regret and genuine compunction with which, till that moment, I could never have credited you. You thought you had hurt my feelings, and you behaved more like a gentleman than I had previously known you to do. You not only apologised, but you also endeavoured voluntarily to make reparation. That produced an effect upon me. You may not believe it, but I desisted accordingly from the trick I had prepared for you.

'I might also have accepted your offer to go to the camel trading post, where I could soon have cleared out, having embezzled thousands. But, then, I should have been in a position of trust and responsibility and I am not quite rogue enough to rob you under those conditions. Whatever else I am, however, I am not a hypocrite. I do not pretend to be anything more than a common swindler. If I return you your papers intact, it is only because I choose to and it had never been my intention to rob you in this manner. Likewise, when I found you had behaved, for once, like a gentleman, contrary to my expectation, I declined to go on with the trick I then meditated. Which does not mean I may not hereafter play you some other. That will depend upon your future good behaviour. If you don't behave, I have a plan to make your name infamous for thousands of years, while your silly little secretary will be acclaimed the saviour of mankind.

'Why, then, did I get Supreme Crown to purloin your dispatch-box, with intent to return it? Out of pure lightness of heart? Not so, but in order to let you see I really meant it. If I had gone off with no swag, and then written you this letter, you would not have believed me. You would have thought it was merely another of my failures. But when I have actually got all your papers into my hands, and give them up again of my own free will, you must see that I mean it. I will end, as I began, seriously. My trade has not quite crushed out of me all germs or relics of better feeling, and when I see a camel dealer behave like a man, I feel ashamed to take advantage of that gleam of manliness. Yours, with a tinge of penitence, but still a rogue, CUTHBERT CONY-CATCHER.'

The first thing Judas did on receiving this strange communication was to bolt downstairs and inquire for the dispatch-box. It had just arrived. Judas rushed up to our rooms again, opened it feverishly, and counted his documents. When he found them all safe, he turned to me with a hard smile. 'This letter,' he said, with quivering lips, 'I consider still more insulting than all his previous ones.' But, for myself, I really thought there was a ring of truth about it. Arugath ha-Bosem was a rogue, no doubt, a most unblushing rogue, but even a rogue, I believe, has his better moments. Nevertheless, in order to ensure that Arugath doesn't misrepresent either my employer or myself to posterity, I have written this narrative of my life and times. This is a true and authentic account of my life in both camel trading and the best brothels in the Roman Empire. Don't believe anything else you hear about me, it will be either a rumour, a defamation or in some other way based on clever forgeries perpetrated by Arugath ha-Bosem.

Yours truly, Jesus H. Christ. Bethlehem 0033 A.D.

ATTACK!

WHERE THE NOVEL HAS A NERVOUS BREAKDOWN

This generation needs a NEW literature - writing that apes, matches, parodies and supersedes the flickeringly fast 900 MPH ATTACK! ATTACK ATTACK! velocity of early 21st century popular culture at its most mEnTaL!

HARD-CORE ANARCHO-COMMIE SEX PULP

We will publish writers who think they're rock stars, rock stars who think they're writers and we will make supernovas of the stuttering, wild-eyed, slack-jawed drooling idiot-geek geniuses who lurk in the fanzine/internet shadows.

HORROR! SEX! WAR! DRUGS! VIOLENCE!

"Subtlety" is found in the dictionary between "shit" and "syphilis".

VICTORY OR DEATH!

The self-perpetuating ponce-mafia oligarchy of effete bourgeois wankers who run the 'literary scene' must be swept aside by a tidal wave of screaming urchin tits-out teenage terror totty and destroyed!

ATTACK! ATTACK! ATTACK!

Hail the social surrealist revolution!